□□□

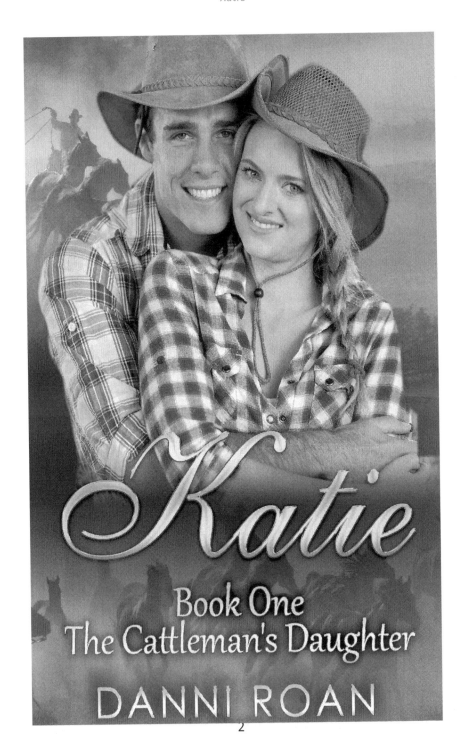

Katie

Book One
The Cattleman's Daughter

DANNI ROAN

Katie
Book One: The Cattleman's Daughters

By Danni Roan

To Jill & Issy,
Thanks for your friendship
Danni Roan

Dedicated to

My two oldest friends, Missy and Ronda, who understood what it meant to ride the trails and still be a lady

Contents

Prologue:

Kansas City, Kansas   June 1880

Will Robertson was down at the heels and down on his luck. He'd finished his turn at driving a big herd up from Texas, just to have the foreman cheat the hands out of half their pay. He was fed up, angry, and tired of working his tail off for another man. There had to be something better.

He looked out across the bustling dusty streets of Kansas City and sighed. At least he had a few dollars, his horse and rig he thought, looking at the red-freckled pony at the hitching rail before him. But how was that going to help him now? Cow hands were a dime a dozen on the streets of this town. He'd be hanged before he went back to Texas with the crew he'd come up with. He had to face it - there was nothing for him; he didn't want to sign on for another trail drive and he wasn't cut out for city life.

He'd just have to see if he could find work and soon, or he'd be plumb broke. He looked at his faded jeans, dusted them off as best he could with his tattered hat, and headed to the mercantile across the street. Maybe someone had posted a job there.

On the other side of the street a large sign hanging above the false-fronted square building read *James' General Mercantile*. Perhaps the owner would know of a place he could get a cheap meal and maybe find a job.

A tiny bell tinkled above the door announcing his arrival as he stepped into the store. The smell of leather, burlap and spices assailed his senses as he stood a moment, letting his eyes adjust to the dimmer light of the interior.

At first it didn't appear that anyone was minding the store, and he took the time to scan the shelves and display tables filling the space. Barrels, crates and burlap sacks lined the front wall under a bright display window. Small square tables were stacked with denim trousers, a variety of shirts, and even boots. A display of small and larger farm implements, brightly colored tins, jars, and bottles filled shelves on the other two walls.

Suddenly, a slim middle-aged woman popped up from behind the tall counter near the rear of the establishment. She must have been reaching for something on the bottom of the floor-to-ceiling height shelves arrayed along the back wall.

"Well, hello there," she said cheerfully. "What can I get for ya?" Her bright smile was contagious and he couldn't help but smile back as he crossed the well-stocked room in a few strides.

"Mornin' ma'am, I'm wonderin' if you know of a cheap place to get some grub, and maybe if there's any work around."

"Come a little closer," she called, waving her hand at him impatiently, "so I can get a look at ya."

He stepped up to the long wooden counter, and for just a moment he felt like a prize bull at auction as her sharp blue eyes assessed him.

"Cowpuncher, are ya?" she asked, almost to herself as she studied him.

"Yes ma'am," he replied quietly, twisting his tattered Stetson in his hands.

"Jeramiah!" she bellowed over her shoulder, making Will jump. "Don't you worry son; my husband will know just what to do with you."

"What are you hollerin' about now, woman?" A man's voice boomed as heavy foot falls crashed down a set of stairs at the back of the building.

"We got a fella needin' work," she yelled back with a twinkle in her eye.

"Oh, we do, do we?" the voice replied inquisitively, just as a tall square man stepped out of the doorway behind her and grinned. For a moment, Will Robinson considered bolting as the man looked at him with a predatory gleam in his eyes. "Well, young man, what kinda work are you looking for?" the older man asked with a smile.

"Ranch work, of course, sir," Will replied, feeling like he couldn't quite get his bearings, even if he had both feet firmly planted on the plank floor.

"That's grand, just grand," the big man boomed. Chuckling, threw an arm around Will's shoulders. "Now why don't you come on upstairs and we'll have a cup of coffee, and you can tell me all about yourself. I think I know just the job for you."

Wyoming Territory   **_July 1888_**

Joshua James stepped out on to the front porch of the ranch house, a big grin splitting his grizzled face. With one hand he tucked an envelope into his breast pocket, then patted it before placing his wide brimmed hat on his head of snowy white hair. For a long moment he gazed around him at the home he'd built - the large barn, the workshop, even the bunk house and chicken coop. He breathed deeply of the early morning air, then patted the letter again. It had been a long time since he'd heard from his brother, Jeremiah. He'd almost thought he might never get the answer he'd been waiting for, but now… He smiled again.

"Morning, boss," a hand said as he walked Joshua's horse to him.

"It sure is," the old man replied, and taking the reins, swung up on his buckskin gelding and started whistling as he turned toward the open prairie. Stopping his horse for the third time on the short ride, he pulled his brother's letter from his breast pocket and read it once more.

Dear Joshua,
June 12, 1888

I believe I've found just what you have been looking for. It should be arriving in about a month's time, hopefully still in good shape. Mabelle helped with the picking and assures me that the packaging is just right; made to order.

We had quite a time procuring such an item for you. The mercantile is busier than ever, but not all items are of the same standard and the choosing had to be done with care.

We are all well here in Kansas. Have you had any word from brother Jonas? I'm sure he is working equally hard at providing you with what you need. Do be patient brother, as times are hard everywhere. Mabelle sends her love to you and the family.

Your Loving Brother,

Jeremiah

Joshua tucked the letter back in his breast pocket once more, then with a smile and a chuckle, started whistling again.

Chapter 1

"Wyoming territory," Will mumbled to himself. He must be plumb loco to ride all the way to Wyoming territory for the possibility of a job. "I've got to be crazy," he grumbled again. His horse twitched its ears, stepping into a trot. Will let his mount set its own pace and watched the trail in front of him.

It had been a strange time in Kansas, and in some ways he was sure glad to be out in the open again. His hosts, Mr. and Mrs. James, had been kind beyond belief, inviting him to stay in their small store room and telling him of work in Wyoming. Apparently, Mr. James' brother was in need of a new foreman and had sent a letter to his brother in Kansas to keep an eye out for a likely young man who could be trusted and was a top hand.

At first Will had a hard time believing it, but Mr. James and his wife Mabelle had treated him so well he felt he owed them something, even if the whole time he was there he'd been peppered with more questions than he'd ever had to deal with in his life. Sometimes he'd felt that if they could have, they would have turned him inside out just to see what he was made of. On the other hand, in the week he'd stayed with them, they'd insisted on providing him with a completely new outfit, explaining that since Wyoming had more cows and sheep than people, it would be hard for him to find new gear out there. They'd gone as far as insisting he take a new pair of boots, and that he could pay them back by filling the position his brother had when he arrived. If he proved himself a hard worker and could make his brother's life easier, that was payment enough.

So here he was, traipsing along the Oregon Trail west of Casper, toward another job on someone else's range. He was twenty-eight years old and had little more than the clothes he stood up in, his old cow pony, Whisper, and the rig he sat on. Will had been working for other men since he was just sixteen and part of him longed for something more, ached for it. Over the years he'd alternately been treated well or he'd been worked to the bone. Some men he'd worked for had been honorable, good men, while others were either too greedy or too stupid to realize how they cheated the men who got the work done each day.

"Well, I reckon whatever happens, I have no one to blame but myself," he grumbled. "I should have learned by now not to be so trusting of folks. But I swear this is it!"

He straightened in the saddle for emphasis, and his wiry red roan horse stepped up the pace. "This will be my last job workin' for another man. After this I'll just get my pay and go find a bit of land for myself." And with that said, he pushed his hat tighter on his head, kicked his horse into a canter, and hoped for the best.

The ranch came into view slowly as the roan gelding stretched his legs in the late morning sun. Will gradually pulled back on the reins, easing his mount to a trot and then a walk as he approached what could only be the Broken J Ranch. From Kansas City he'd taken the train to Cheyenne, and then rode into Casper. The fledgling city was just getting going with a new railhead spurring its growth and was a bustle of cow country fare. From Casper, he followed the directions given him by the livery man in the little town.

He'd been traveling this trail for nearly four days now, and was sure pleased to finally see buildings in the distance. Setting his horse back to a quick jog, he studied the land around him as he rode. Wide-open prairie surrounded him, stretching out from the trail on all sides, grass lands rolling as far as the eye could see. In the far distance a blue haze indicated where the mountains were, but everything else was prime cattle territory.

Slowing his horse to a walk as he got closer to the ranch, he noticed the care that had been put into the fenceline that surrounded the spread. It was the first thing to interrupt unbroken prairie for at least a hundred miles. A sturdy wood rail fence stretched for nearly a quarter of a mile both east and west, encompassing the ranch yard and buildings completely. Right in the middle of the fence, two tall poles topped with a sign that read *The Broken J*, the J itself almost split in two by a jagged arrow, marked the entrance to the property.

Will let his mount amble through the high arch as he tried to take it all in. On his left, a tall windmill turned lazily in the morning breeze, pumping water into a cistern at the far corner of a corral, while several horses milled about nibbling hay in the barren stock yard.

A large barn, weathered gray and two stories tall, rose to his right. Its straight lines and steep pitched roof showed fine workmanship and care. Next to the barn he spotted a smithy, smoke puffing from its chimney as the ring of iron on iron punctuated the air. Off in the distance, on the other side of the trail that passed between the barn and main house and extended all the way through to another arched entry, was a long dark building which must be a bunk house. He even spotted an old sod shack tucked in the far corner, as well as a smoke house and chicken coop.

But what truly drew his eye was the large, two-story ranch house of wood and stone on his left. It had a long, low porch that seemed to wrap around the entire structure and its steel-gray wood blended with the stone foundation and facade. A tall river rock chimney reached from the first floor to the second and took up half of the north face of the house, while the top of another seemed to rise on the south. At the front of the building, above the low porch roof, four glass paned windows framed by heavy oak shutters gazed across the barnyard, while under the shadowed depths of the porch a thick door, complete with a screened door, in the center of the house was skirted by two more windows. The whole structure was topped with a galvanized roof over both the porch and main house. It was a fine looking place, and not at all what he had expected of Wyoming. Maybe this trip would be worth it after all.

Turning his mount toward the house and swinging down, he tossed his reins over the hitching post at the bottom of the stairs and prepared to go to the front door. He'd no sooner loosened the girth of his saddle to give his horse a breather, when the screen door opened and a very tall old man stepped out. He was a big man, at least six foot three and broad in the shoulders. His hair was stone white and his eyes, in his weathered face, a piercing blue. "You must be the new foreman?" the older man stated gruffly.

"Yes sir," Will replied.

"Well, I'm Mr. James, and you sure took your time getting here." The older man's words were terse.

For a moment, Will could only gape at him. Was the man serious? He'd gotten here as soon as he could without killing his horse. He thought he'd made good time covering the eight hundred plus miles in under a month.

"Well nothing to do about that now," the white-haired giant grumbled. "You might just as well get on out on the range. You can see the dust from here, so shouldn't be no problem finding the round up."

Will gazed across the prairie in the direction the old man was looking and could clearly make out a dust cloud being kicked up by what must be the cattle. He hesitated just a moment before looking back at the old codger and offered a stunned "Yes, sir." To his surprise, the old man grinned.

"Take your horse on over to the barn, and Sam will see to him." And with that he went back into the house, letting the screen door slam behind him.

Will unwound the reins of his horse, Whisper, and turned to the barn, feeling like someone had placed a burr under his saddle. As he entered the cool confines of the spacious stable, the familiar clop, clop of horse's hooves met his ears. A short, thin man with a completely bald pate grinned at him and handed the reins of a handsome bay to Will while taking his horse from him.

"Howdy," the wiry fellow said with a nod. He turned and walked away, taking Will's horse with him.

Will shook his head, adjusted the stirrups on the new mount's saddle and walking back into the bright sunlight, swung aboard. The big bay, feeling Will's weight in the saddle, humped his back to show him that he was feeling fresh, but before he had a chance to really get to bucking, Will slapped spurs to the animals flanks and lined him out at a dead run through the gates of the ranch. He turned west toward the maelstrom in the distance. If this was the way it was going to be, he'd just have to show the lot of them he knew his trade, and the sooner the better.

Joshua James stood at the window of his ranch house and chuckled. He watched the young man lay spurs to that ornery bay and string him straight out to work. The boy had grit.

"You're an old devil," a woman's voice chided as a dish cloth descended upon his arm with a light smack.

"Now Bia, there's no point puttin' up a fuss. How else am I going to take the measure of that young man if I don't test him?"

The old housekeeper looked at him and smiled. "I know Josh, but the poor boy hasn't got a clue what he's just stepped into," she said in heavily-accented English.

"That he don't."

Chapter 2

Will let the big bay ease down into a fast canter after about a half mile. He wasn't far from the dust now, and was able to make out a green and white chuck wagon on the outer edges of the roundup. The cattle themselves were blurred shadows of sunlight and dust, emerging one minute just to be engulfed again the next by a cloud of their own making.

In the distance he could see cowpokes milling about on horseback, getting the herd settled or dodging out after a mossy cow that was thinking of cutting loose. He counted maybe ten hands in different positions working the herd, then watched as a palomino pony darted out of the dust, quickly turning a large red steer back into the main herd. His critical eye noted the rider, glued in the saddle and upright the whole time, as the cow horse dodged and danced, pushing the animal back where it belonged.

Will cantered up to the chuck wagon and hauled the bay to a stop as the big animal shook its head and snorted in protest. Several men hunkered around the small cook fire, drinking coffee and eating off tin plates. As Will approached the group, a bear of a man rose up from where he sat turning dark, weathered eyes on him. The man was big, well over six feet and easily three hundred pounds of muscle, but Will could see that age was starting to take its toll. The big man's back, once straight, bowed a little, his hands were worn and scarred, and the hair under his hat was more silver than black.

"Howdy," Will called. "I'm Will Robertson, the new foreman."

All of the heads at the fire turned to him as one by one the men stood. He noticed that not a one of these men could be under fifty and for a moment felt foolish about his earlier words.

"I'm Benjamin Smith," the big man said, extending his hand. "I'm the OLD foreman," he drawled, shaking hands, as everyone around the fire burst into laughter.

Will looked at them all, a warm blush creeping up his neck, turning his ears pink. Then he noticed that the face of the grizzled old bear who had spoken was smiling, and he smiled, too.

"What took ya' so long getting' here son?" he asked, a twinkle still in his eye.

Will just looked at the man, his mouth hanging open like a fool, and the whole group howled with laughter again. A slow smile made its way across Will's face, as the joke finally sunk in and he couldn't help but chuckle, too.

"Sit down, Sonny," cried another man. His wispy white hair stuck out from under a gray, sweat-stained hat, as he grinned toothlessly while wiping his hands on his apron. "Reckon you could use some grub. We're about to go round two here now," he added with a significant look at the other men still standing with plates in hand. The men quickly wolfed down their food, handed him their plates and with a nod stepped up to their ponies.

"Sit down, boy," Benjamin indicated, picking up his plate as the old cook handed one to Will. The cook went to a metal triangle hanging from his wagon and clanged it with his ladle before turning back to the fire.

Will sat and started shoveling grub into his mouth as fast as he could. The beef and beans sure tasted good after his long trek, and he wasn't wasting time. He'd almost finished his first plate when the thunder of hooves caught his attention and the same palomino he'd seen earlier came charging toward the chuck wagon, its golden coat shimmering in the sun. Despite the dust its white mane and tail were brilliant. The rider wore a bandana wrapped around the lower part of his mouth to ward off some of the dust of the roundup, but strangely had another wrapped around his head under a wide hat as well. Will watched the posture of the rider and how he handled his horse, if perhaps a little recklessly, still well, as the little golden horse came skidding to a stop.

There was something strange here, though. The rider, garbed as the other hands in boots, trousers, chaps and flannel shirt, was rather short and didn't seem to sit his horse in the same way most cowboys did. The rider threw a leg over the saddle horn and slid off the horse onto small-booted feet, pulling the bandana from his nose and down around his neck. Will jumped to his feet and stared in utter shock as the rider approached the fire. He blinked a few times, still unable to speak from the shock. This rider was not a cowboy; this rider was a woman.

"Where's the grub, Cookie?" a lilting voice called as the woman walked to the cook fire, brushing dust off her shirt and chaps with each step. Her denim pants were baggy but still showed all too clearly the curve of her hips as they swung when she walked.

"Cookie?" The girl called again, now looking up from removing her gloves to see why the toothless old man hadn't replied. She noted the eyes of the cook gazing across the fire, and began to turn.

"Uncle Benji, what in thunder is wrong with Cookie?" Her voice trailed off as she saw Will. "Oh," she squeaked. "Excuse me. I didn't realize we had a guest." She turned her full gaze on Will and her ice-green eyes sent a shiver down his spine. "Um. Mr." she said, looking right at him. "You're spilling your beans."

With an effort, Will pulled his eyes from her face to look down, and sure enough his plate was dripping beans onto the fire. Suddenly a wild cackle broke out behind him and everyone turned to see the cook doubled over, holding his sides and laughing.

"You done shoulda' seen your face," he cackled. "Looked like you been plumb pole-axed." Then he was off again, consumed by laughter.

Will shook himself with an effort, then snatched his hat from his head.

"Ma'am," he said, still gazing at the girl across from him. She'd been wearing the bandana over her nose and mouth and he noticed she had the distinct look of a raccoon as the area around her eyes was dusty, but her skin below was clean and smooth. She wore her hair in a long braid down her back and it shone like wild honey in sunlight, not quite red, but not golden either.

She was the prettiest thing he'd seen in a long time and he couldn't take his eyes off of her. Just then the sound of more approaching riders caught everyone's attention, but he couldn't drag his eyes away from the woman who was still smiling at him. Two more riders approached the fire and sidled up to the woman.

"Katie?" another female voice called out. Will whipped his head around just in time to see two more women step up to the girl already there.

His mouth fell open further and he stood gaping like a fish. The cook's mad cackling snapped him out of his stupor.

"Ma'am-s," he greeted weakly.

"Katie, what on earth is going on here? I'm starved," the second girl said.

"Apparently Pa hired a new man," the girl called Katie replied. "Meg, Fi, meet Mr...?" She paused. "I'm afraid I don't know your name," she ended politely.

"Robertson, Ma'am. Wilson Robertson."

The cook still hadn't stopped laughing, but somehow managed to dish up two more plates and brought tin cups full of coffee to each of them. The women joined the men at the fire and sitting down just like all the other hands, began to eat.

"Uncle Benji?" the first girl, Katie, asked. "Did you know about this?"

"Course I knew. I been your pa's foreman for more'n twenty years. You don't think he'd let me out a' somethin' like this, do ya?"

Will sputtered and almost choked on his coffee. This girl, and by the looks of it, the other two, were the daughters of the old, cantankerous cattlemen who'd hired him. Was this a complete mad house?

"Why do we need a new foreman?" the second woman, Meg, piped up in a sweet voice. She was about the same height as her sister, but was leaner and more angular, with a wide set to her shoulders and a narrow waist. Her hair was a coppery red with hints of sunlight streaking it and she had eyes of aquamarine.

"I ain't gettin' any younger, you know, Meg," Benji replied. "We'll need a younger man to see to the next drive. I'm thinking it's time for me to start takin' it a little easier around here."

"Oh, Uncle Benji," the oldest girl, Katie, scoffed. "You'll be driving cows 'til they carry you away."

She turned her startling eyes on Will, who suddenly found it hard to swallow. He'd been studying each girl in turn, and wondered how in the world he'd ended up sitting around a chuck wagon fire with three women. It all just didn't seem possible.

"Have you ever worked as a foreman before, Mr. Robertson?" she finally asked.

"Yes, ma'am," he stated flatly. "I've been driving cows up from Texas my whole life, and did just about any job that needed doing on a ranch. I'll do my best at whatever you need here." He didn't notice the two older men's conspiratorial smiles.

"Did you come all the way from Texas for this job?" The youngest girl, Fi, finally spoke for the first time. She had darker hair than her sisters, a deep chestnut brown with hints of gold glinting in the sunlight. Like her sisters, she wore it in a long tight braid down her back, but unlike them, she wore no bandana under her hat.

"No, ma'am," he replied politely. "I'm comin' up from Kansas just now. I heard about the job there."

"Oh!" Fi gasped. "Did you meet our Uncle Jeremiah?"

Will smiled. "As a matter of fact, he's the one who suggested the job to me."

Just then another horse came trotting up to the fire and the old man from the ranch house swung his large frame down from a big buckskin horse.

"What ya all doing lollygagging' around the fire? Don't you have work to get on with?" he asked tersely. The three girls giggled but the three men stood, slapped their hats back on their heads and turned toward their mounts.

"You'd best come with me son," Benjamin said softly, and pulled Will along with him.

The rest of the day was spent doing what usually happens during a roundup - branding, checking stock, and culling weak or sickly cows and calves from the herd. Will, despite the weariness of his long journey, worked next to Benji, putting in a full day's work. Occasionally, he'd lift his head and spot that fast-moving palomino horse charging off to chase down a stray or drag a reluctant calf to the branding fire, and he couldn't help shaking his head. *What kind of crazy old man had his own daughters out herding cattle?* He noticed that all of the girls, once he could spot them, were doing a man's work and that the hands never once went to help them out any more than they did the other cowpokes.

As the sun started to reach the western peaks in the far distance, a new group of cowboys came out to relieve those who'd worked all day. The new watch would get the cattle bedded down and look after them for the night while everyone else turned toward the ranch.

"Time to call it a day," Benji sang out. "You just stick with me."

So together they turned their tired mounts toward the east. Will noticed the girls riding together in the lead with their father while he, Benji, and the other men brought

23

up the rear. He was sure gonna be glad for a meal and his bed roll tonight.

As they approached the ranch he watched the girls head straight to the ranch house. The bald man from the barn scurried over and took their horses with a grin and headed to the barn. Will and the other men all turned toward the corral and began to dismount, stripping the gear from their horses before turning them out. He noticed his roan horse nibbling hay contentedly with the other mounts and turned toward the bunk house.

"Where you goin' son?" Benji's voice pulled him up short.

"The bunk house," he replied.

Benji's chuckle surprised him. "Not yet, you don't. We take our meals at the big house."

Will pulled his hat off of his matted hair, looked at his sweat and dust-encrusted clothes, and gulped.

"Don't worry, you can clean up with the rest of us," Benji said, chuckling as he began to amble in the direction of the ranch house with Will on his heels. Will thought they'd walk up the stairs onto the wide front porch but instead they started around the right side of the house where they found the rest of the day shift, stripped to their trousers and washing in a big basin of warm water. Some were even going as far as to dunk their heads straight into the trough before stepping to the side and pulling down a sheet of toweling to dry off. They shook out their shirts, put them back on, and headed around to the back of the house.

When it came his turn, Will shucked off his shirt, grabbed the soap and plunged his head in the water. He scrubbed his face, neck and hands as best he could, then dried himself on a towel, combing his dark brown hair out of his eyes with his fingers.

"You clean up alright boy," Benji said. "Can't wait to see what you look like after Saturday's bath."

And again he and the other cowboys burst into laughter, slapping the younger man on the shoulder and heading for the back of the ranch house.

"No, you go bring, coffee!" A woman's low voice drew Will the rest of the way around the house, and he wondered if he were going to meet the mother of the three girls from earlier.

As he made the turn around the corner of the house, he could see two long tables had been placed down the length of the house and were quickly filling up with ranch hands. A short plump woman with salt and pepper hair stood by the door holding a long wooden spoon in her hand, shouting into the interior of the house, and a muffled reply could be heard coming back to her. She was dressed in a deep gray dress with a high collar trimmed in white lace, and her brown eyes sparkled. She smiled as he and Benji took their hats off and ascended the stairs.

"Oh!" She squealed seeing them. "Look! Look! We have a new one. And so handsome, too." She waved them to a table with her spoon and turned back to yell into the kitchen again. "Hurry up! Hurry up!"

"I'm coming, I'm coming," a high male voice with a strange accent called back. The voice was accompanied by a small, wiry Chinese man carrying a large coffee pot. "You too bossy," he said, glaring at the woman who simply rolled her eyes and gestured with her spoon.

Benji, smiling the whole time, led Will to where Mr. James sat at the head of a long trestle table that could easily seat twelve. Benji walked around to the bench where four old cowhands sat, and indicated for Will to take the seat next to him, while he took the one to the left of his boss. The bench on the other side of the table still sat empty, Will noticed.

The noise and clatter of dishes and utensils, along with the banter between the house matron and the Chinese man, who seemed to be trying to outdo each other in grumbling, created such a cacophony of noise that Will almost missed it when Mr. James asked to say grace. But Benji heard and bowed his head, then one by one all of the cowboys bowed their heads as well. A sudden hush fell over the back porch and the old man lifted his voice.

"Lord, for this food which we are about to receive, may we truly be thankful. Bless us with your bounty and bless the hands that prepared it. Amen."

He lifted his head and grabbed for a piece of fried chicken on a plate in front of him before passing it to Benji. Just as the men had started piling food on their plates, the wide screen door screeched open on its hinges and not three, but six girls marched out one by one as all of the men stood.

The first one was Katie, now dressed in a green day dress with a softly rounded white collar, followed by Meg, then Fi. These three he had met at the chuck wagon, but then behind them came two more girls who were obviously identical twins. They had dark brown hair and bright hazel eyes, and tittered to each other as they marched around the table to sit with the men. The last to arrive was a petite girl with jet black hair and a small heart-shaped face. Her dark eyes were full and wide, but with a turned-up shape like a cats. Each girl walked up to Mr. James, gave him a peck on the cheek, and sat in order of age along the far side of the table, directly across from Will and the other men. All the old punchers sat back down while Will just stood gaping.

"You gonna stand there all day sonny, or are you gonna eat," Mr. James groused.

Will plopped back down on his seat, feeling a deep blush cover his face. Benji elbowed him and grinned but turned back to the food. Finally over his shock, Will filled his plate and began to eat his well-earned dinner while his eyes kept straying to the row of woman seated across from him. Unlike his earlier encounter, where three of the girls were working cattle dressed as men, now all of them wore simple day dresses and had put their hair up instead of leaving it in a long braid. All but the youngest, anyway, whose inky tresses hung loose down her back. They were all as pretty as a picture.

"I know you met my three eldest earlier today," Mr. James stated brusquely "But let me introduce you properly. You've met Katrion, my oldest, then there's Muiread, and finally Fiona. Next to her are Isabella and Alexandria."

Here the twins interrupted. "But call us Issy and Lexi," they said hastily, while their father raised an eye brow in reply and carried on.

"And last but not least is little Mae Lynn." After each girl was introduced, they nodded politely before filling their plates.

"So how did you find your first day?" Katie asked, looking across the table at Will.

"It was alright; seems everyone knows how to work around here," he replied with a smile. The younger girls giggled.

"Now Katie, leave the man alone. He's tryin' to eat," her father said.

"We heard you came all the way from Texas," one of the twins chimed in.

"Did you?" the other asked.

"Um, no ma'am. I came from Kansas City."

"Girls," their father's stern voice warned again. Just then the lady of the house approached with a big plate of biscuits, and Will started to rise again.

"Oh, none of that now, boy," The woman chided, and placed the biscuits on the table.

"Bianca, have you met our Mr. Robertson yet?" Mr. James asked "Bianca here's my mother-in-law, Mr. Robertson," he added as the woman shooed him away again.

"Joshua James, you're gonna scare this boy away with all this talk. He's hardly eaten a thing so far, and you know how confusing it can be around this place for strangers. Now let him concentrate on eatin' his dinner and he can get us all sorted out later."

"Bianca," a wiry little man at the other end of the table called. His once black hair was now dusted with gray, but his dark brown eyes still held a twinkle. "Don't you go nosing into Joshua's business! Come here and sit down like a good wife, and leave the men to their eating."

"That's Isadoro, Bia's husband. They're from Italy," Benji whispered, "but don't try too hard to keep track, you'll get used to it."

The rest of dinner was a melee of conversations, questions, and quips from the men at the table. Will decided that unless someone spoke to him directly, he'd be better off just watching and taking in the lay of the land, but as the meal wore on, the only thing he was sure of was that Mr. James had six daughters, and that Isadore and Bianca were Joshua's in-laws.

The conversations were so jumbled and confusing, he wasn't even sure of the rest of the hands' names by the time he'd cleaned his plate. Finally, the meal ended with a large chocolate cake and coffee before the men excused themselves, wished the woman a good night, and headed to the bunk house.

Chapter 3

Will's head was still spinning as he walked with the other hands to the bunk house. He found his saddle bags and bedroll already there on one of the bunks, and without even thinking, he plunked himself down on the cot, still dazed. Benji came over and sat down next to him.

"You alright son?" he asked gently, a half-hidden smile on his face.

"I've just never been anywhere like this before," Will replied. "Is every place in Wyoming like it?"

"I doubt you'll ever find a place quite like the Broken J, anywhere," was Benji's easy answer.

Will shook his head and looked around the bunk house. It was a low-squat building with thick log walls, and from where he sat, Will could see that the building had two main rooms. The one he was in had bunks lined up along all four walls except near the door, and looking through the open door to the other, he suspected it was a mirror image of this one.

A large table with a selection of battered chairs and a potbellied stove was situated in the middle of the rectangular space. Against the wall near the door was a tall cupboard with a set of cups and a tin of coffee on its bare plank shelves. Above each bunk was a small shelf with a few pegs stuck in the wall beneath it, and he could see that the men had placed some of their own personal items there. He also noticed that most of the beds were made up and the majority of them had a large square wooden trunk or box underneath them. Overall, it was a snug place with enough space to allow men a bit of privacy, but without being so big it couldn't be kept warm in the winter.

Removing his hat, he hung it on the peg above his bed and ran his hands through his thick, dark hair. Once again he took a look around him, this time counting cow hands. There were seven altogether, although he knew there were a few still out on the range, and the most striking thing about the whole crew was that not a one of them could be less than twenty years his senior.

"Why don't you get settled?" Benji told him, rising and heading to the long table. "You've had a long ride, and a longer day. Give it all a little time to come together in your mind. I'm sure you'll feel better after a good night's sleep. Besides, tomorrow's that last day of branding so things will settle down."

Will spent the rest of the night hanging up his one change of clothes, and putting his gear, what there was of it, away. Finally, he washed up at the basin by the door and crawled into his bed roll. Tomorrow would come early and he was tired, but as he drifted off to sleep instead of thinking through the next day's work, a vision of a pretty girl with honey-colored hair danced before his eyes.

Dawn found Will once more on the back porch of the sprawling ranch house, eating with the hands. The ladies were nowhere to be seen, but the noise was not decreased in the least by their absences.

The old Chinese cook stumped his way around the table on bowed legs, placing stacks of pancakes, baskets of bread, and platters of ham and bacon on the table with a thump, then poured coffee into any cup he deemed to be not quite full.

"That's Joshua's other father-in-law." Benji whispered with a nod toward the wizened man.

Will felt his eyes go wide.

"Well, I guess really he'd be his great father-in-law. Josh married Chen Lou's granddaughter. She was Mae's mother." In a louder voice he called, "Chen Lou, you old coot, can't you see my cups almost empty over here," he added in gest, lifting his almost full cup.

Chen Lou stomped around the table to where Benji sat, his long white braid swaying with every step of his skinny bowed legs. He wore a strange outfit that looked like a light loose jacket over trousers and small slippers on his feet. He poured coffee for Benji with a grumble, but smiled warmly at Will, bobbing his head.

Will couldn't help but think the whole ranch was not only totally confusing but rather strange. How did a man like Joshua James end up with an ancient Chinese man as a father-in-law and kitchen staff?

As the sun crept over the horizon, bathing the deck with a golden glow, the ranch hands began rising one by one and making their way to the barn and to their mounts. Seeing Benji stand, Will rose to his feet, but Mr. James waved him back to his seat.

"You stay here with me a while. The boys (an ironic term if Will had ever heard one) can finish up with the branding. We'll have a little chat, then I'll show you round the place properly."

"Yes, sir," Will replied as Benji patted him on the shoulder before leaving with the other men.

"Where you from?" Joshua James asked, turning his arctic blue stare on Will.

"I'm from Virginia, well what's now West Virginia, originally," Will stated, "but my folks moved out to Missouri after the war. I've been moving cows from Texas for most my life though," he replied.

"Your folks still livin'?"

"No, sir. They've been gone a long while now."

"Got a' sweetheart back in Missouri?" the white-haired man asked inquisitively.

Will started at the questions but decided to reply anyway. "No sir, never had time for a sweetheart, not with dustin' the trails all the time." Will squirmed under the bright gaze of his new boss.

"I've been here a long time now, son. Came out in '68 and settled right here. Lived in that little soddy yonder with my wife and baby girls."

He gestured in the direction of the earthen shack Will had seen the day before.

"Made this place into something with these fellas who came with me. Twenty years now I been raisin' cows here, and frankly I'm getting' tired. Things are changing fast. The last two winters just about did us in, and cattle won't be king much longer if you ask me. We fared a lot better than most being here in the basin, but it was rough." He paused for a few moments thinking, and continued, "I believe that it won't be long until Wyoming is granted statehood and then think of what will happen. The railway's made it to Casper, and soon this whole area will be full of people. I need some new blood around here if I expect this ranch to keep goin'. Someone who can think ahead and find a way to keep this place a float. Diversify.

You think you're up to the job?" He finally ended, his Viking eyes boring holes into Will.

"I'll do my best, sir," Will said, swallowing despite himself. "I've had enough ramblin' to last me a life time already. So if you're lookin' for a fella to stick around and see this place grow, I think I'm your man."

Will was startled when Mr. James reached his large hand out across the table. "Glad to have you then," the old man said and shook Will's hand with gusto. "Now let's get you a tour of the place."

Chapter 4

Katie finished dressing for the second time that morning. Snapping the last button on her white blouse into place with a disgruntled huff, she smoothed her beige riding skirt so that the wide divided sections fell together like a regular skirt.

She'd rather be in her denims and on the range again today, but her father had asked something more of her. She wondered for a moment if she would see the handsome puncher again, but quickly put the thought out of her mind. If her father was true to form, he'd keep the young man as far away from her and her sisters as possible. There'd been a few young punchers pass through on the ranch before, but they'd been kept well away from the James girls.

The new hand was all her sisters had talked about after dinner the night before, but she knew how it was on the ranch and that as likely as not he'd be on his way before long. Sighing, she examined herself in mirror. Nona Bianca had come to put her hair up for her earlier, taking her time and fussing over Katie as if she were a princess. It was nice to be girlie for a change.

Although technically Bianca Lioné was the biological grandmother of Issy and Lexi, she had been a grandmother, Nona, to all of the girls at the Broken J over the years. Katie smiled, admiring the intricate knot Nona had made of her hair. It had been a long time since the older woman had found the time to fuss over Katie. It would be a shame to cover it up with a hat, she decided, giving her hair one final pat, before turning to head downstairs. She'd no sooner stepped from her room then Mae came charging by and raced down the stairs. Katie rolled her eyes and followed.

Joshua James pushed himself to his feet in preparation to start his day when the back door swung open with a loud bang, and his daughter Mae came storming out.

"I do not need a babysitter!" she exclaimed without even a good morning to her father or his guest. "I am perfectly able to go riding by myself," she added, crossing her arms over her small frame and tilting her chin defiantly.

Almost on her heels, but minus the dramatic entrance, came Katie, her glossy hair up in a most becoming way, and seeing her, Will whipped his hat from his head, nodding politely.

"Don't need a babysitter hey?" Mae's father quipped, one eyebrow raised in question. "Do I need to remind you of what happened last time you went haring out across the prairie on your own?" he asked, raising an eyebrow at his obstinate off spring.

"Oh, Pa," Mae moaned. "I'm old enough to be out by myself for a little ride. There's no one around for miles and miles. What could possibly happen?"

"You could," Katie stated from directly behind the much smaller girl, causing Mae to whip around with a glare.

"Your sister's going with you today and that's final," Joshua stated, his tone making it perfectly clear that no argument would be accepted. "As a matter of fact," he added, looking at Will, "I think you girls can do me a big favor today. I was just going to take Mr. Robertson out and show him the spread, but since you're riding out anyway why don't you just take him along with you and I can go see how the last day of branding is progressing?"

"Oh," Katie started, surprised that her father would send the young man out with his girls. "Well, if it will help."

"It sure will. What do you say, Mr. Robertson, is that alright with you?" Will looked first at the two young women, and then at his boss.

"Yes, sir," Will replied. "Sounds like a dandy plan to me." He couldn't help but note, however, how Mae's face became even stormier, and without another word she turned and stomped back into the house, her small boot heels setting a loud staccato pace. Katie was right behind her.

"You'd best get a move on, son," Mr. James chivvied "That girl won't wait for no one."

Snatching up his hat, Will dashed through the still-open screen and into what was obviously the kitchen, a room that took up the whole back section of the house.

"You need this!" the Chinese cook called, holding up a heavy sack that he handed Will as together they quickly scurried down the long central hallway past the stairs and out the front door.

Four horses stood tied at the hitching rail, including his red roan, but he'd barely had time to register the scene when Mae leapt into her saddle, turned her calico pinto south, and raced full speed from the yard. Katie, a heartbeat behind, swung up onto her palomino and turned after her sister with a groan.

Still clutching the heavy bag, Will thrust a foot into his stirrup and before he'd even hit the saddle, had Whisper after the girls. The lean, long-legged red roan stretched out over the rutted trail, eating up the distance between him and the horses in the lead. Will quickly came abreast of the lithe golden mare, only having a moment to take in the look of sheer determination on Katie's face as she leaned over her mount's neck, pushing for more speed. The roan, finding his stride, surged past as Will gave the gelding his head. Lying low of the animal's neck and whispering in its ears, Will's eyes quickly teared with the rush of the wind, and soon he was neck and neck with the Mae's smaller pony.

Leaning precariously out of his saddle, Will grabbed the bridle of the little pinto and began hauling on the reins. His roan, sensing what he wanted, began slowing his pace, forcing the other horse to do the same. They'd no sooner come to a stuttering halt then Mae threw back her head and howled with laughter. Her long black tresses were tangled with the string of her hat, and her cheeks were rosy with the thrill of the ride. Will was just thankful the child hadn't broken her fool neck.

"Mae Lynn James!" Katie's excited voice exclaimed as she pulled her horse to a sliding stop beside them. "You could have killed yourself or one of us running off like that. You should know better! What if something had happened to Mr. Robertson?" She asked, trying to bring her trembling voice under control.

For just a moment a shadow passed over the young girl's face. "You hurt, Mr. Robertson?" she asked quietly.

"No."

"See, no one was hurt," the girl called, "and besides it was fun. Of course you've forgotten what that is," Mae retorted, not noticing the hurt expression on her older sister's face. "Did you see his roan run, Katie? That's about the fastest horse I've ever seen. Can I ride him?" she added excitedly, now looking at Will.

"Mae!" Katie exclaimed in shock at the rude question.

The younger girl rolled her eyes and shook her head, turning her pony on down the trail. "Alright, alright. Let's just show him around, then," she cast over her shoulder, and kicking her mount into a trot, set off.

Pulling her horse up alongside Whisper, Katie looked at Will as they both moved out to follow her impetuous sister. She noticed, somewhat to her surprise, that the man didn't even seem to be angry at her little sister, but by the twinkle in his eye had found the whole thing rather exciting himself.

"I'm sure sorry about that, Mr. Robertson," Katie ventured. "Mae's, well Mae's just Mae. You can't hardly keep her still for a minute and everything's a big adventure to her. I hope she didn't startle you too much," she offered apologetically.

"It's alright, ma'am, Whisper here didn't mind stretching his legs," Will said, patting his horse's neck. "He likes a good run now and then."

Noticing the sack still in his hand, Will raised it with a questioning look to Katie who groaned.

"That will be our lunch. I hope it isn't ruined," Katie offered with a shrug. "I guess it will just depend on what was packed," she added, eying the sack skeptically.

Pulling up for just a moment, Will turned in his saddle and put the sack into one of his saddle bags hoped for the best before turning and trotting after the receding figure in the distance.

"Any idea where we're going?" he finally asked as they jogged along a ragged trail.

"Mae loves to explore, which means we could end up anywhere. The best I can say is that at least her pony has an unerring sense of direction when it comes to getting her home."

"Do you have to do this very often?" Will asked, gesturing with his hand toward the small form riding ahead of them.

"We've all had to take a turn, though I haven't had to for a long while. Usually Issy and Lexi ride out with her, at least since the last time she put herself in a fix."

She sighed heavily and continued, "Last year after she turned thirteen Mae convinced our father she was responsible enough to go out on her own, so he let her. When her pony came ambling into the barnyard on its own later that afternoon, we knew he'd made a mistake. You see, Mae can't seem to think things through. If she has a thought in her head, then the next moment she'll be doing it. Apparently, she thought it would be fun to crawl into a badger's den and see if it had any kits."

"Fortunately, it was an abandoned den, but she got stuck in the narrow tunnel, so after waiting a while her pony just came on home. Every one of us turned out to look for her. Pa was beside himself. Ever since then, he won't let her ride out on her own."

Will couldn't help but smile at the tale, though he could see how at the time it must have scared her family half to death.

"Well, Pa said I should show you the spread, so I'd best start pointing things out while we keep an eye on Mae," Katie said after a moment of awkward silence. Then she started describing the place she called home.

Chapter 5

Joshua James stood on the back porch listening to the sound of racing horses and shook his head with a smile. Placing his white Stetson on his head, he stepped off the porch and walked to the large oak tree on the corner of the fenced property.

Walking under the dark cathedral of its overhanging branches, he removed his hat and ran a hand through his still thick, snowy hair and bowed his head over one of the three larger head stones sheltered in its shade.

"Well Bridgette, my dear," he spoke softly, his deep voice not even loud enough to disturb the birds in the branches above. "I've started, just like I promised I would. I'm doing the best I know how for our girls and I'll see them all settled before I join you. It would have been easier if you'd been here. You'd know what to say to them. I'm afraid I let them grow up a little too much maybe, but it's so hard thinking of them leavin'." For a moment his voice faded as a lump rose in his throat. "Everyone's pitching in to help. I even have my brothers helpin' out. Now we'll just have to see what happens. Keep an eye on them from up there if you can," he added, looking heavenward. Placing his hat on his head once more, he turned and walked back into the bright morning sun.

Again and again Will's eyes were drawn to Katie's face as she animatedly explained the points of interest around them while they rode. Her tawny, flame-

42

kissed hair had loosened from its intricate coif, and soft strands lay around her face, framing it. Her stunning eyes were lit with a passion for the land she obviously loved.

Over and over he would follow her gloved hand's direction as she pointed out a rise, or indicated where a spring or stream ran behind a copse of trees, but steadily, as if pulled by some invisible string, his eyes would turn toward her face, tracing the soft curve of her cheek, or becoming absorbed in the deep pink tint of her full lips.

It was apparent from the time she began schooling him on the ranch that she had a deep love of her home. She was knowledgeable, intent and quite direct about each benefit or short-coming of the ranch. He was surprised to learn that the spread was much larger than he had expected, and that at the moment they ran nearly twenty thousand head of cattle, a small miracle after the blizzards of '86 and '87 that had decimated the state over the past two years.

He was also shocked to find out that each and every hand who worked the ranch owned some part of it, whether simply having claim to some small piece of the land itself, or sharing in the profits of the ranch as a whole. It made sense; in a strange way, each man would want the ranch to be as successful as possible and would, in turn, reap the benefits of their own labor. It certainly explained why there were so many older hands on the place.

"Across that draw..." Katie's voice pulled him back from his thoughts and once again his eyes roamed her delicate features. "...is Uncle Benji's spread." She pointed to a low rise backed with tall pines, a field of grass spilling downward along the hill to the prairie below, and a small brook bubbling and bouncing its way into a larger tributary on the flat land.

"It's all part of the whole but when he decides to stop ram-rodding for Pa, he has a nice little cabin there."

For a moment their eyes met as Katie looked directly at him, and a strange warmth seemed to creep from his middle and spread up and down his whole frame. It had been a long time since Will had actually looked at a pretty woman and unsolicited, the thought that he wasn't getting any younger roared through his head.

"Hm?" Will caught himself asking.

"Mr. Roberson, are you paying attention?" Katie asked, looking at him more closely.

"Yes, yes of course," his voice was a heavy rasp as it scratched across his throat. "It's just… it's just a lot to take in at one time." *Was she blushing?* Will wondered.

For a moment time seemed to stand still as Katie looked up at him, eyes wide, lips slightly parted, breath coming in shallow gulps. Will wanted to kiss her. Longed to reach out and place his large callused hands in her silky tresses.

Clearing his throat, he broke the spell, turning his eyes back to the high distant mountain range. There was no doubt about it, he'd been alone too long and there was no quicker way to get run off this ranch than to start looking at the rancher's daughter like a love-sick pup. He would have to watch himself, especially if he had any hopes of getting a bit of this land for himself.

"Darn!" Katie's soft expletive shocked him to the tips of his boots and he turned gaping at her.

"Sorry," she said her face a light shade of crimson. "I can't see Mae anywhere."

Will felt like repeating her mild curse as he began scanning the low foot hills they were approaching.

Kicking their mounts into a brisk trot, they headed out in the direction that the erstwhile Mae had been traveling, and before long they came across the tan and white calico pony tied to a low growing creosote bush, his black tail swishing lazily in the late morning sun.

"Mae?" Katie called looking around. "Mae, where are you?" Her voice had taken on a desperate edge.

"I'm right here," came a disgruntled-sounding voice, followed by the girl herself, stepping from behind a small clump of trees and buttoning her light jacket.

"What do you think you are doing running off like that?" her older sister chided. "What if something had happened to you?"

Mae rolled her eyes. "I needed the necessary," she smirked. "It's not like it's just you and me out here, you know," She turned a significant glare on Will.

"Oh." Again Katie's cheeks flushed, and it was all Will could do to suppress a smile.

"I'm hungry!" Mae interjected. "Let's go down by the creek and have lunch." Without waiting for a reply, she untied her pony, mounted, and turned westward without a backward glance.

Katie sighed, shook her head, and swung her horse in the direction her baby sister had gone.

Half an hour later, Will found himself sitting on and old blanket next to Katie, under a cottonwood tree, eating fried chicken and munching on a somewhat shattered apple pie. Near them Mae sat nibbling her food, her back turned toward them as if willing them away, while she watched a babbling brook gurgle and tumble over large smooth stones. The low green slopes of the foot hills of the Wind River Range spilled onto open prairie, dotted with the deep hues of tall evergreens or thick-limbed cottonwoods that grew along the banks of the brook.

In the far distance, Will could see mule deer and antelope grazing in the lush grass as granite peaks reached their gnarled summit toward a pristine, blue sky. Will had been asking Katie questions about the ranch, and she had been answering them while keeping an eye on her sister. He had still been studying her face when he noticed her eyebrow raise in alarm as she started to get to her feet.

"Mae?" she called sternly, "What do you have?"

Mae tried to turn her back further, but then her sister was looming over her. Will, curious, followed and looked down just as the young, raven-haired child was trying to stuff something back into her jacket. No sooner had she pushed it into the folds along her waistline, then a small black and white head popped back out, its beady black eyes gazing up at the intruders. In just the nick of time Will clamped a hand over Katie's mouth, stifling the scream that was rising in her throat.

"Shh," he whispered, never taking his eyes off of the fuzzy bundle that came tumbling out of Mae's coat. The tiny creature leaned down and took a delicate bite from the chicken leg in Mae's hands. Katie, now calmer, pushed Will's hand away.

"Where in the world did you get that?" her shocked whisper came out a squeak as her finger pointed at the white-striped baby skunk in her sister's lap.

Mae at least had the sense to look abashed but didn't hesitate to reply. "It was in a hole and couldn't get out." Her words tumbled over each other in a cascade. "It was making the most terribly sad noise. What could I do? I couldn't leave it there to die." Her eyes were plaintive.

Katie closed her eyes, breathing slowly through her nose to maintain her calm so as not to panic the black and white urchin who was still calmly eating Mae's lunch. Swallowing, she spoke with more decorum than she felt.

"Mae, you can't keep it. You need to turn it loose."

"But why?" Mae asked, confusion plainly etched on her face.

"Because it is a skunk and if for any reason it were to get startled… it doesn't bear thinking about."

"Oh." Mae's face fell and her eyes lingered on the tiny creature that had now cuddled into her lap. "It's just so tiny and all alone." Bright tears glistened in the girl's eyes.

"I know, but it needs to be with its mother." Katie's voice was now soft, gentle. "We'll take it back to where you found it and leave it there with some food. I'm sure its mother will come for it."

Mae simply nodded, wrapping the little bundle in her hands and tucking it back into her jacket.

Mounting up again, they all turned back toward where they'd come from. Soon Mae was standing by the same creosote bush she'd tied her pony to earlier and placed the little skunk, with a healthy helping of chicken and pie, in its sheltering branches. Katie wrapped her little sister in a big hug afterward and softly wiped away her tears.

"He'll be happier here, Mae," she whispered. "Now let's head home."

Silently, Mae mounted her pony and turned toward home.

The ride back to the ranch was subdued. It was obvious that Mae was taking the loss of the little polecat hard, and Katie felt like the bad guy once more. It was hard being the oldest in this family. Mae was so full of life and compassion, imagination, and dreams. Why was it that Katie always had to be the one to step in and squelch it? As the oldest she'd had to look after her sisters; she knew she was too serious, too bossy, but if she didn't take things seriously who would?

This ranch was everything. She was a very part of the land, the sky, the grass. It pulsed in her like a second heartbeat. The snort of a horse next to hers brought her out of her depressing thoughts and she looked up to see Will Robertson gazing at her.

"You alright?" he asked tentatively. For a long moment Katie was unable to answer, shocked not only that he would ask, but by the intensity in his deep hazel eyes.

"Um, yes," she replied softly.

"You did the right thing you know." Will's words were gentle. Katie looked up at him and smiled.

"Thank you. I know I did the right thing, but I didn't want to hurt Mae." She watched as her sister trotted along a short distance ahead of them.

"Sometimes it's hard to be responsible," was Will's simple reply, and for some reason it did something strange to Katie's heart. A warmness seemed to surround it, wrapping it in a soft glow.

The rest of the ride home was completed in silence, but it wasn't awkward or strained. Each of them rode cloaked in their own thoughts as their horses plodded along toward home.

As the trio approached the entrance to the ranch, Mae kicked her tri-colored pinto into a gallop and dashed through the archway, skidding to a halt at the hitching rail. The sound of galloping hooves had brought the old Chinese cook to the door, but Mae, tears in her eyes, dashed passed him and on into the house.

Will heard Katie sigh as they swung down at the front of the house and looked up at the disgruntled face of Mae's great-grandfather.

"Kat-tri-on!" He snapped "What you do to upset Mae?" He glared down at her his dark eyes, fierce as he rested his hands on his narrow hips.

"I…" Katie stammered.

Suddenly Will felt fiercely protective of the woman standing beside him and he had to clench his fist to keep from reaching out and taking her hand.

"She only did what was right and what needed doing," he said before he could stop himself. "She didn't want to hurt Mae. She was just looking out for her."

For a moment, the old man glared at Will, a scowl on his parchment face. Then Will watched as the old man shook himself, his whole body sagging. "What did she do?"

he finally asked in resignation. "Do I need to go see her now?"

Quickly Katie sketched out what happened, and to Will's surprise the old man doubled over with laughter before turning back toward the house.

Katie turned to Will and just looked at him for a long moment. Her steady eyes on his face made his cheeks warm as he smiled down at her. Then he remembered himself, and reminded himself that he was just a hand on this ranch and that this was the owner's daughter, putting a check on his feelings.

"Ma'am," he said calmly. "I'll just take the horses back to the barn if that's all you need for now."

"Oh," Katie whispered, handing him the reins of her mount, then watched him stride toward the barn, the two horses at his heels.

Wearily Katie trudged up the stairs to her room. She was hot and tired and feeling very confused. She just wanted to find some time to sit and think, but she needed to make sure that everything was alright at home, check to see if the final roundup and branding went well.

She wondered if her father had worked the rest of the day or if he was just checking stock. She knew that as the oldest daughter her responsibility was to the ranch, to seeing that it continued to prosper and support her sisters. Her father was getting on in years. How much longer would he be able to keep this up? She had to take care of him.

Her mind drifted to the cowboy she'd spent the morning and afternoon with. At least her father was starting to hire some younger men to take on the heavier work. *He's handsome, too.* She pushed the stray thought away.

Still completely engulfed in her thoughts, she turned the knob on her bedroom door and pushed it open only to find both Meg and Fi waiting for her.

"We thought you'd never get back," Meg called excitedly waving a hair brush. "Nona says you're to have a bath and we came to help. Now tell us everything. What is the new cowboy like? Where did you go? Why was Mae upset? Don't you think this new fella is handsome?"

Before Katie could even begin to respond the twins entered, filling the room almost completely.

Katie raised a hand to stave off the onslaught just as Nona arrived, carrying a bucket of steaming water and poured it into the half full tin bath sitting on the floor.

"You had nice ride?" she asked, her accent stronger than usual for some reason.

"Yes," Katie replied, somewhat confused about all of the fuss.

"Good, good. You must be hot, take nice bath and have a rest before supper. Yes?" Patting Katie on the cheek, she left the room, latching the door behind her.

With a deep sigh, Katie began unbuttoning her blouse. Her sisters rushed to help, battering her with questions about Will the whole time.

"Oh, Katie," Meg finally gushed. "What if he falls in love with you and you get married?"

"Meg!" Fi chided her dreamy sister. "Leave her alone."

"Meggie, I know you have dreams of love and marriage and all of that, but you're younger than I am. I'm already twenty-four and well past marriage. Don't be silly. Besides I have enough in my life with this ranch and all of you. What do I need with romance?" she finished as she undressed and stepped into the tepid water with a sigh. Katie leaned back into the tub, allowing the warm water to wash away the dust and tiredness of the day.

Picking up the hair brush again, Meg smiled wickedly at her sister. "Then I guess I'll just have to marry him."

A strange cold feeling slowly slipped into Katie's stomach and her eyes flashed back at her sister in the mirror. "Do what you want," she said, her voice terse.

To her surprise, Meg collapsed in peals of laughter on the bed. "I don't want him. He's too skinny for my taste." Again she cackled wildly, making Katie and Fiona shake their heads.

"Maybe Fiona will have him," Meg finally rasped out between extended giggles.

Rolling her eyes, Katie climbed out of the bath, wrapping a heavy towel around her.

Fiona, who had taken the brush from Meg, began working on smoothing and drying Katie's waist length hair, flinched. "He's far too old for me," she finally whispered, which set them all off to laughing.

Strangely the whole thing seemed to relieve Katie's worries about the ranch and her father, and she could feel a lightness in her she hadn't had in a long time.

Chapter 6

Over the next several days, Will threw himself into his work, keeping close to Benji and learning the ropes of the Broken J. He hoped that long days in the saddle and hard work would put a pretty face and a pair of jade eyes out of his mind, but each meal put him face-to-face with the girl again.

Still, he was determined to show his worth as a top hand and hoped that if he proved himself worthy, a piece of the ranch itself could be his. He spent his evenings talking to Benji and the other hands about the ranch, coming to understand how each had earned their part of the share. Most of the men had been on the Oregon Trail with Joshua, and when he'd decided to stop here in Wyoming, they had chosen to stay too.

At the long dinners he answered the questions of all of the girls, as well as Joshua James, and began to notice just how serious and worried Katie seemed to be. Her soft face often drew into a frown as she questioned her father about the preparations for the drive to Casper's brand new railhead. He knew she, Meg, and Fiona had been working the roundup as well, and was impressed by her tenacious attitude.

Will had been on the ranch for nearly three weeks, working himself and his horses hard, and getting things done. Rising to a gray watery dawn, he dressed and slapped his hat on his head before heading to the back porch and breakfast.

At the table, he and Benji got down to going over the plan for the day while they waited for Joshua and the girls to make their appearance. In just under two days the herd would head down the trail to Casper and the trains that would take them to the big cities back east. The cattle had been bunched and culled, and the breeding stock and young stuff had been driven out to the best grazing land in preparation for the winter. Will was looking forward to ram-rodding the drive and seeing it completed.

Nearly all the food was already on the table by the time Joshua and his daughters arrived. Katie stepped onto the porch boards close on his heels, still arguing some point in a loud whisper, but as they rounded the corner of the table, the rest of the family strung out behind them like ducklings in a row, Joshua James wheeled and faced his daughter, his face grim. Katie just had time to come to a stop before slamming into her father's wide chest.

"Katrion-Blakely-James." He pushed the girl's three names out between clenched teeth. "I've told you how it will be and that's how it will be. You're going and I'll have no more argument."

"But Pa…," Katie tried plaintively, "Meg…"

Joshua stopped her with an uplifted hand. "No. You're going and that's that."

An awkward silence fell over the whole porch as all eyes watched the interaction between father and daughter. Finally, Katie dropped into her seat with her face a storm cloud. Joshua sat, said grace, and picked up his fork. As he and the rest of the men began eating a hearty breakfast of biscuits, saw mill gravy and eggs, he turned his eyes to Will.

"I've a special job for you today," he said without preamble. For just a moment, Benji's eyes strayed to where Isadoro and Bianca sat at the end of the table.

"Yes, sir," Will addressed Joshua, ready to take on the next job.

"I need you to see Katie safely up the mountain to my brother-in-law Brion's place. He's not doing well and sent a message down asking for some supplies. I have everything ready, so you'll need to get a move on pretty quick if you want to be there before sundown. I'll trust you to keep my Katie safe on the ride." The big man's piercing blue eyes bored into Will's.

"Yes, sir," Will said again, trying to control his features so that utter shock was not evident. Briefly he looked across the table at Katie's storming face, and understood her frustration. Still, he simply nodded and dug into his breakfast.

As soon as his plate was clean, Will followed a tight-lipped Katie through the house, out on to the front porch, and down the stairs to where their horses, along with two pack horses, stood waiting for departure. Katie, dressed in her dungarees, chaps, and a flannel shirt, threw herself into the saddle of her familiar palomino horse, her jeans making a soft slapping sound as her bottom hit the seat, and without a word she turned toward the hills in the far distance.

Will, still a little shocked, scrabbled to take up the lead lines of the two pack horses, then leaping into his saddle, turned to follow her.

For the first hour Will followed behind the rigid form of the girl on the golden horse. He noted her stiff shoulders and straight, tense back as she kept her horse at a quick walk. Finally, he pushed his roan up beside her, catching a softly grumbled word as he matched her pace.

"He did this on purpose, you know," she said, not really talking to him but needing to vent at the same time. "I told him I was going with him this year on the round up, so he's dreamed up some excuse to keep me home."

She was quiet again for a while and Will, instinctively realizing she just needed to talk, kept quiet.

"I'm the oldest, I have a right to see that things get done. I have responsibilities." Katie's voice was soft.

Soon the gray sky became more overcast and fat rain drops began to fall. The two riders stopped to pull their rain gear off the back of their saddles, but continued on their way toward the mountains. The horses, used to traveling in all sorts of weather, kept up their steady pace as they pointed their noses toward the far blue hills.

"How far's your uncle's place then?" Will finally ventured as the wind began picking up, turning the steady rain first one direction and then another.

"Oh, yes, you don't know do you? Well he's just at the edge of the Wind River Range. It will take us most of the day to get there."

Suddenly Will realized just why Katie had been so angry. The whole crew was mustering out the next day to start the drive toward Casper. There was no way he or Katie could possibly be back in time to leave with them. Pondering the thought, he first wondered if he'd done something to upset Mr. James, something that had made him decide to have Will escort Katie instead of leading the drive. Then he wondered if he simply thought that as the newest and youngest hand, he could just catch up with the drive later on. Either way, the whole thing was odd. He looked up to see Katie's eyes on his face.

"Now you get it," she said, her tone wry. "I guess there's nothing to be done now but get to Uncle Brion and go from there."

Will noted the resignation in her face and smiled despite himself.

"Yep. I reckon that's all we can do," he said, and tilted his hat to shed more of the water away from his neck.

More clouds, black and billowing, rolled toward them over the distant mountains and by midafternoon rain was coming down hard. As they approached the foothills to the tall Rockies, the weather worsened and rain lashed at them as they rode, driving rain under slickers and around collars.

Soon they were both shivering and the storm not only showed no signs of lessening, but distant thunder indicated that a real storm was brewing in the big mountain range. Will was beginning to worry and started looking for likely places to shelter in the foothills. Soon they were trotting their horses into the pelting rain, trying to reach the shelter of the trees and hoping for an overhang or cave. Thunder crashed above them as he guided Whisper into the pines and they steadily climbed. The thick branches of the pines lessened the impact of the rain but deepened the gloom, bringing almost total darkness.

Straining his eyes, he scanned along the tree line for a break in the mountains above. Suddenly, Whisper began turning toward a dark outcropping of rock, and with great relief Will let the pony pick its way into a deep recess in the rock. Behind him the pack horses moved restlessly as Katie, shivering in her saddle, pushed her little mare up next to them.

Will stepped down from the dripping horse, then reached up to help Katie out of her saddle. He noted that she was shivering all over, and as she slid off of her horse he wrapped his arms around her to steady her. She leaned into him, her head coming to rest just under his chin.

"I'll get some blankets and start a fire," he said, gently pushing away from her. Outside the meager shelter, thunder crashed against the mountain and lighting back-lit the horses standing huddled together at the entrance of the cave.

Will pulled the bedrolls from the saddles as rain dashed across the mouth of the overhang, and quickly brought them to Katie, draping them both around her shoulders. Finding some dead wood further back in the cave, he quickly started a small fire. It wouldn't be much, but it would be a start. As the wind picked up and lightning flashed, Will pulled his hat down over his eyes and, hunching his shoulders, stepped out into the storm.

Heading back into the trees, he dug under the low branches of the pine trees, breaking off dead limbs that were kept dry by the thick green needles above. Little by little, he gathered arm loads of smaller branches, then began picking up larger ones. It wasn't much, but would have to do.

When he returned for the last time, he saw that Katie had a battered enameled coffee pot sitting on a rock next to the flames. The light reflecting from the sandstone walls painted a rosy glow on her face, and he stopped to catch his breath before he could move forward. Placing the wood near the fire, he turned back to the horses and began stripping their tack. Katie looked up from the fire to see what he was doing.

"I don't know how long this storm will last, so I might as well make them as comfortable as possible," he said in answer to her questioning look. A nod was her only reply.

Unpacking the horses, Will carried the gear and heavy packs toward the back of the semi-circle of rock that protected them from the storm, then walked over to the fire to warm his hands. Katie went to the saddle bags and packs and pulled out a skillet and provisions for some hot food.

"We might as well have something hot in us if we're going to have to stay here," she said to him, her head bent to her task. Will smiled, pleased that she wasn't falling apart as the storm raged.

Katie rummaged through the panniers for supplies. There was bacon and a few loaves of Nona's long, slim loaves of bread. She could make some hot bacon sandwiches, and soon she had the bacon sizzling in the pan. Going through the motions of something as familiar as cooking bacon steadied Katie's nerves.

What in the world had her father been thinking, sending her out here with a storm on its way, and with this man who was a virtual stranger? It would have been different if it had been one of the other men, men she'd known nearly her entire life.

Soon the sooty, salty smell of bacon was filling the little space they'd found for shelter. The curving walls of the cave were perhaps twelve feet in circumference, with a wide mouth and a heavy overhang jutting out into the darkening day. The front of the cave was just tall enough to stand up in, but it tapered upward as you moved further back, and she was forced to stay bent over the fire while she cooked.

Every now and then she would look up to see Will standing near the mouth of the cave looking out at the storm. He'd taken his hat off and shaken most of the water from his dark hair, which curled and twisted around his ears and along his collar. She could see that his shirt was damp as it peeked out of the turned-down collar of his rain slicker. His jeans below the knee were damp and his boots muddied; hers were no better. Turning back to the fire, she tore open a loaf of bread and began laying strips of crispy bacon into the fold, allowing a liberal amount of the drippings to be soaked up by the bread.

"Food's ready," she finally stated, holding out one of the sandwiches. Will turned away from the entrance and stooping a little, walked to the fire, folded his tall frame onto the floor of the cave, and took one of the sandwiches.

"Thank you," he said, looking up into her bright eyes and biting into the warm sandwich. Katie handed him a cup of coffee and sat down as close to the fire as she could.

"We'll need to get out of these wet clothes," Will said between bites, his eyes now on the fire. "There just isn't enough wood to dry us out."

"Yes, I see what you mean," Katie replied slowly, munching through her own bit of bread and bacon, her eyes wide with the thought of having to change her clothes out here in the middle of nowhere with a man nearby.

"It just makes good sense," Will stated, trying to put her more at ease. "When we're done with this," he gestured with the bread in his hand, "I'll just step out and you can change."

"But that means you'll be soaked through again." She paused for a long moment. "Why don't we just use a blanket as a curtain and change behind that." Her voice was matter of fact, though it quavered at the end.

"Alright, if that suits you."

When they finished their sandwiches, Will picked up one of the blankets and stretched it behind his back, making a wall from his out stretched arms as he faced toward the entrance. Katie dug out a change of clothes she'd found in her saddle bags and quickly shimmied out of her wet trousers and shirt. No matter how hard she tried she could not suppress the deep blush that warmed her cheeks at the thought of being this close to the handsome young puncher in next to nothing but her camisole and knickers. As quickly as she could, she pulled the warm, dry clothes on and buckled or buttoned with madly scrabbling fingers.

"All done," she finally squeaked.

Will lowered the blanket behind him, letting it fall to the floor and swallowed hard. The sounds that had been coming from behind that blanket had left his mouth dry. He'd found Katie attractive since the first time he'd laid eyes on her, but the thought of her stripped nearly naked just inches away from him had made every nerve in his body pulse. Keeping his eyes down, he took his turn while Katie held the blanket at her back.

On inspection of the improvised wall, he wasn't sure that it was actually very effective, but at least it gave some sense of propriety to the situation. Shucking off his boots, he crawled out of his wet jean, pulled his still half-buttoned shirt over his head before yanking the dry clothes back on, and stomped into his boots. He had to admit he was much warmer, but wasn't entirely sure if it was due to the dry clothes or from the heat coursing through his system.

"That's better," he finally spoke so that the girl standing with her back to him could relax. Again, heat coursed through him as she let the blanket fall, affording him a view of her bottom covered in loose fitting jeans. He found himself swallowing hard again, then with a weak smile he stepped back toward the entrance of the cave to check the horses and let the cool, damp air cool his face.

He felt, more than heard, Katie walk up next to him as he gazed at the storm outside. "It's not letting up, is it?" she asked softly.

"Afraid not."

"My uncle's place is still hours away from here," she almost whispered.

"I'm afraid we'll have to bed down here tonight, then," Will's voice sounded flat event to his own ears. Another peel of thunder punctuated his statement.

With no sign of the storm letting up, Will and Katie set about making up their beds. Darkness had fallen hours ago, but with the driving rain and roiling black clouds it was hard to tell the difference.

Will couldn't help but notice that Katie was efficient in all she did. She didn't waste time with worry or fear; she just got on with the job that was needed. Still, he knew she had to be uneasy about spending the night alone in the mountains with him. He wracked his brain trying to think of any way to put her at ease.

Katie rolled out her bedding, absorbed in her own thoughts. It was full night now and there was no sign of the storm lessening. These early summer storms could wreak havoc on the ranch and she hoped that everything was alright. Again, she wondered what in the world had possessed her father to send her away at this time. Perhaps Uncle Brion was in really bad shape, but if that was true why hadn't he come down the mountain? Worry creased her brow as she chewed her bottom lip impatiently. She had hoped to get to her uncle's cabin and then head back to the ranch the very next day. She was sure she'd be able to catch up to the cattle drive if she were only a day behind.

"How long will it take us to get to your uncle's cabin once the storm breaks?" Will's rich voice interrupted her troubling thoughts.

"Huh?" she said, startled.

"I was wondering how long it would take to get to the cabin."

"Oh. Well, as far as I can, guess it will take about four hours from here. Maybe a little less. We'll probably have to stay another night there, though, because even if we just dropped off the supplies, we couldn't make it back to the ranch before nightfall."

"That's going to make it hard for me to catch up with the drive to Casper, then," Will spoke without thinking. Noting how Katie's eyes had gone wide, he stood up from where he'd been leaning against the cave wall and gazed around him looking for what had startled her.

For a long moment, Katie was struck dumb by the fact that the man standing across the fire from her had echoed back her own thoughts.

"You're worried about the drive too?" she finally questioned softly.

"Well, yes, of course." Will's thoughts felt muddled as he gazed into the pale green eyes of the girl looking at him. "I'm to be the new foreman, and the first drive I'm here for I'm high up in these forsaken mountains instead of down there seeing that the job is done and everyone gets through safely." He couldn't keep the frustration out of his voice.

Katie, emboldened by his words, stepped around the fire and came to stand directly in front of him. "Uncle Benji's not getting any younger," she said. "He needs to start settling some of the work on others."

"I know," Will said, running a callused hand through his dark hair in frustration. "I've been trying to take things over a little at a time. He's been teaching me how things are done at the Broken J, but he can't keep it up forever. For that matter, none of the men your father has on the ranch are young. Every day I see the toll the work takes on Benjamin. That's why I don't understand why I'm up here. Just about anyone could have taken these supplies up the mountain." Katie's soft gasp stopped him.

"Oh, I'm sorry ma'am, I didn't mean any disrespect to your Pa. It's just…"

"I know." Katie's soft voice and bright smile brought his words to a stumbling halt.

"I feel the same way. I can't imagine what Pa was thinking. Any of my sisters could have come up, and he could have sent just about anyone to do it. Now it has me wondering what Uncle Brion's message said. I just get so frustrated sometimes."

Her eyes flashed as she looked at him intently. The passion in her voice glowed on her face, and for a moment threatened to take Will's senses.

"I've spent nearly my whole life on this ranch," Katie continued. Will could sense that she needed to talk, and determined to listen. "It's everything." Her voice picked up again as she gazed toward the pitch black mouth of the cave.

"I was only four when we came here. I barely remember the wagon train or anything other than the little sod shack we built. Pa, Uncle Brion, Uncle Benji, Deeks, and several of the other men all agreed to just stop here on their way to Oregon. I almost remember my mother's joy at finally having a home."

She paused again, her voice taking on a faraway sound. "Muiread was only two and Mammy was carrying Fiona. I used to help her in the soddy as much as I could. I knew that as the oldest I had responsibilities. I'd keep Meg busy and help make sandwiches for Pa and my uncles." She paused again as her thoughts roved back over her childhood memories, dredging up joy and pain alike.

"Mammy died after Fiona was born." For just a moment her eyes drifted back to his. He could see the sorrow within them, mixed like the flex of gold among the green in her gaze. "I did my best to take care of Pa and my sisters. It was a God-send when Nona Bianca and Grans Isadoro came. Fi was tiny, and sick too; she was only six months old."

"Nona and Gran's wagon had broken down, and the wagon train they were with just left them. Pa and some of the other men found them trying to make their way back to Casper and brought them home." A soft smile stole across Katie's face as she remembered the day she'd met her new

65

mother. "Their daughter, Camilla, was with them. She was so beautiful. She married Pa that next year and became our new mother."

Again Katie turned her eyes to Will's. He wanted to reach out and touch her, the joy and sorrow in her voice pulling at his heart. "Of course we lost her to a fever several years later. In some ways that was harder for me than losing my own mother. I could just barely remember my mother; I didn't get the chance to know her like I did Cammy."

"Grandpa Isadoro is the one who started the ranch house we live in now. He built most of the structures on the Broken J. He's a real master builder. He learned wood-working in Italy as a boy." Her voice was full of pride.

"Pa and the other men had been farming the land, but the year Cammy and her parents arrived, they decided to get cattle and start ranching. I had to help Nona and Cammy and keep everything going while the men went to buy the herd."

For a long moment, Katie's voice faded. A branch collapsed and crackled in the fire, sending sparks toward the rock above their heads. Will waited, not breathing, not saying a word.

"Before Nona and Grans came, Meg and I went everywhere with Pa. We rode horses, plowed fields. It's not like he could leave us at home. Billy took care of Fiona. He had a goat and that's what saved her. After Nona and Grans came, we still spent a lot of time out in the fields learning how to do work while Cammy took care of Fi. I remember the day they came back with the cows," she said with a smile. "Four hundred head of cattle they moved from Texas. Pa was thrilled. We still had to do a lot of farming, and Pa and Brion even brought timber down from the mountains and hauled it to Casper. We all did our part. That's how I learned to work the ranch, filling in when someone was away." Her eyes took on a fiery gleam, a spark of pure determination.

With the mention of her uncle's name, Katie stopped, slowly coming back to reality. "I don't know why I'm going on about all of this," she sighed heavily. "Right now we're stuck right here, so we might as well just make the best of it." She looked up at him, and without thinking, Will reached out a hand and brushed a strand of soft, damp hair away from her face, sending a mild shock racing up his arm. Katie closed her eyes and leaned into his hand. Remembering himself, Will yanked his hand away, leaving it feeling suddenly cold and bereft of heat. Katie's eyes flew open and with a gasp she turned away, stalking back to the fire.

"We'd better get some sleep," she snapped, bending over and crawling into her bed roll.

Will stood rooted to the spot, looking at the stiff back of the woman lying on the floor of the cave, her thick golden braid reflecting the colors of the fire. Mentally he cursed himself. What had made him do it? What could he possibly have been thinking? He had only wanted to comfort her, to take away some of the worry she was feeling. Silently shrugging into his slicker, he turned toward the mouth of the cave and stepped into the storm that crashed and rolled outside, hoping to escape the one that raged inside his soul.

Chapter 7

"I hope you know what you're doing." Joshua James groused at Benji as he paced the kitchen floor.

"Trust me. They'll be fine," Benji called back over his shoulder as he watched the steady rain fall outside. The storm had moved in quickly. What had looked like just a steady rain had turned itself into a deluge in no time at all, and he and Josh knew it would be far worse in the mountains. He hoped that Will Robertson and Katie had made it to Brion's cabin, but in his gut he also knew there was no way they could have made it there in time.

"That boy's sensible and savvy. He'll find a shelter for them and keep Katie safe."

Joshua continued his pacing, pausing occasionally to glare at the back of his longtime partner who stood, infuriatingly calm, hands tucked in his back pockets, staring out at the darkening night.

"He sure seems the type to take care of her, I can't argue that, but you know how those mountains can be."

"Jeremiah and Maybelle did their job well," Benji replied as thunder rolled through the valley. "We both agreed this was the way to go, Josh. That boy was doing his best to stay away from Katie and that's not the plan. He has some fool notion that looking at your girls will get him the sack. You know it. I know it. The only ones who don't know it are the two stuck up there on that mountain somewhere."

"At least we know he's an honorable sort," Joshua replied grudgingly. "Who knew we'd have to practically hog-tie them together. You'd think two young people would just sort of gravitate toward each other. It's only natural."

Benji's soft chuckle echoed in the quiet kitchen.

"You two still worrin' bout them young ones?" Bianca's voice interrupted their thoughts as she hustled over to the cook stove and stoked the fire. "I make coffee. Sit, sit."

She chivvied them with her hands and both men turned toward the table. Joshua noted the way her accent had reemerged, which only happened when she was upset. A few minutes later, Isadoro joined them as his wife put cookies and coffee on the table and turned up the lamp.

"We were just saying how it sure is hard work to get them two youngin's together," Benji said, sipping the dark brew.

Joshua nodded. "You'd think they didn't like each other," he said with a grimace.

"Oh, no, no, no." Bianca wobbled her head determinedly. "I watch them. That boy has eyes for our girl and it's just a matter of time." She reached out and took her husband's brown, gnarled hand in her plump one and patted it.

"Katie, too," Isadoro added his brown eyes smiling mischievously. "She just can't let go of the ranch. She still thinks she has to take care of you, Josh. That girl needs to learn to live and stop trying to take care of everyone else around her. "

"She needs to start listening to her heart," Bianca added.

"I just hope she's safe out there," Josh said, turning toward the window and the night outside.

"We will pray for them," Bianca stated, reaching for Benji's hand on the other side of her as she bowed her head.

***

A drop of cold water trickled down Will's neck, sending a shiver along his spine. He'd been scrounging fire wood under the thick pines, and for the most part they kept the rain off of him, but every now and then one fat droplet would find its way under the collar of his slicker. He'd gathered several arm loads of semi-dry wood already and was headed back to the cave.

He could just make out the soft flicker of light from the small fire as it cast the horses' shadows into grotesque shapes that danced in the driving rain. Entering the mouth of the make-shift shelter, he studied the horses as they dozed where they stood. Quietly, he stacked the wood near the cheerful blaze. Taking off his rain gear, he slipped between the blankets of his bed roll and let sleep find him.

Will's first inkling of trouble was a snort from his horse, Whisper. The fire had died down, so the first thing he did was to add a few branches to its meager flame. Dark shadows crept around the cave and the horses began fidgeting.

Will reached across his saddle and pulled the Winchester carbine rifle from its scabbard, his eyes scouring the mouth of the cave as the horses became more restless. He heard Katie climb from her blankets and begin walking to their mounts, talking in soft calming tones.

Suddenly all four horses whirled, pushing and bumping into each other, bolting from the cave entrance as a tall shadow raised itself up with a snarl. The huge grizzly made a mad swipe at the fleeing horses, narrowly missing the rump of the last animal through the entrance. Will raised his rifle and fired. The huge bear swayed on its hind legs but didn't topple as Will worked the lever action of the gun. The bear, now injured, snarled, dropping to all fours and lunged for Will, as white froth sprayed from its mouth around razor-sharp teeth. Will fired again, and the bear staggered but kept coming. One more time the click, click of the carbine's action snapped and with another deafening boom, it fired again. The bear collapsed all at once, but its forward momentum slammed it into Will's legs, knocking him to the floor.

Dazed, he tried to push the dead animal away as he distinctly heard the sound of another gun being cocked. Straining, he looked up to see Katie standing over the bear, a large pistol at the ready.

"I'm alright," he croaked around his adrenaline-tightened throat and began pushing at the huge weight that had settled on his legs.

Katie, placing the pistol on the cave floor, walked over to him and bit by bit they pushed the bear off of his legs. Rising, he studied her face, noting the wide eyes and gray color around her eyes and mouth.

"You alright?" he asked gently.

She only nodded, then bending, helped him roll the carcass to the mouth of the cave, before sagging to her knees by the fire. Quickly, Will went to her. Now that the crisis was over, her whole body was shaking and tears danced in her eyes. Sitting beside her he gently wrapped an arm around her and pulled her close. She didn't resist; she just sagged into him and began to cry.

"You were great," he whispered into her hair as he rested his cheek on her head. "You were so brave. You didn't even scream." Against his side, warm and soft, Katie sobbed. "Shhh" he crooned. "It's all over now. You're safe. We're safe." He just kept repeating the words, holding her close to his wildly beating heart until her sobs had stopped.

Somewhere in the early hours of the pre-dawn, Will felt Katie slip into sleep, but he couldn't bring himself to let her go. All through the long hours of dawn he held her close to him, feeling the heat of her body soaking into his heart. She was amazing. He'd known woman who would have collapsed at the first sight of a monster like the one outside, but Katie had held it together until she knew he was safe.

As the first golden rays of the sun pushed the rain away, he finally woke her. For a moment she was confused, then gasped as she realized she'd fallen asleep in his arms. Slowly, gently, reluctantly he separated from her, purposely not looking at her face for fear he'd give in to his need to kiss her.

"I'll have to go find the horses," he finally croaked. She nodded beside him, eyes still down-cast. "Will you be alright here by yourself?" She turned wide, startled eyes at him that flickered toward the mouth of the cave and the gray lump that was brightening with every minute.

"No. no. I mean yes. No I mean, we'll go together. If we're lucky they won't have gone far."

He smiled. The girl had pluck. "Alright." He looked at the now hours' cold fire and sighed. It sure would have been nice to have a cup of coffee before leaving, but there was no point waiting. "You ready?" For the first time that morning, Katie met his eyes. A soft blush rose across her cheeks, though he wasn't sure if it was due to their closeness throughout the night or the gentle glow of the rising sun. She gave one nod, picked up her pistol, and started for the exit.

They tried tracking the horses as they wound their way down the side of the mountain, but it was no good; the animals had raced through underbrush and across rocky ground, leaving only tell-tale signs.

Eventually they just traipsed to the bottom of the hill and to their surprise, found Whisper contentedly munching grass at the trail's end. Will whistled at first sight of the tall gelding, causing the red-freckled animal to lift its head, whinny in reply, and trot toward them.

"Now aren't you a sight for sore eyes," he said, smiling and rubbing the horse's forehead. The long reins of the bridle trailed behind the horse and Will scooped them up. He turned, grinning at Katie as she patted Whisper's neck.

"I'll give you a leg up, and then we'll head back up the mountain," he said, offering his hands as a stirrup. She tucked her little booted foot into the sling made by his palms and swung up, scooting toward the big horse's withers and gripping his mane.

Will placed a hand on the horse's shoulder and in one smooth motion swung up behind her. "We'd better just head toward Uncle Brion's place," she called over her shoulder as he began guiding them toward the trail. "If he knew we were coming, he'll be worried and without the other horses someone will have to come and get the tack anyway."

Will nodded his agreement and turned the roan in the direction she indicated, trying to ignore the distraction of her warm body pressed against his as they rode. He kept moving to adjust his seat to keep a respectable distance between them, but with each stride of the horse his body would ease up behind hers, and soon a heat that had nothing to do with the steadily climbing sun at his left filled his body. If the close contact was bothering Katie at all she didn't show it, but instead began pointing out interesting landmarks nearby.

Here the mountains were crisscrossed by streams and tributaries to the Wind River and more than once he found himself urging Whisper to splash across a stream. At one point the tough mountain horse tripped and stumbled for a moment. Instinctively, Will's hand snaked around Katie's slender waist, pulling her in to his chest to keep her from slipping from their mount's bare back. She didn't resist, but instead allowed herself to lean into him. Will sucked in a sharp breath as his center began to warm. The gentle step and slide motion of the horse forced him against her rump, making more than his sense of propriety uncomfortable.

Katie found herself letting go. Just this once, while no one was around to judge her, she would enjoy the moment. She reveled in the feeling of the man pressed against her back, his warmth spreading across her tense shoulders and giving her a sense of peace.

When the horse stumbled and Will's hand had claimed her waist, she leaned into him, letting him hold her upright in front of him. Where his hand rested, liquid fire began seeping along her body. She shivered with delight, which made his grip tighten.

She knew it was wrong, knew she shouldn't be so close to a man she wasn't married to, but she also knew that at her age she would never marry. Will was protecting her, keeping her safe, that was all and for the moment she would allow someone else to watch over her.

As long as she could remember, there was someone needing her to take care of them. First her mother when she was so sick waiting for Fi to be born. Then when her mother was gone, she was responsible for Meg. She had to look out for her father and help him. She had responsibilities to the ranch, to her family. But today, just for a little while, she would allow herself to be a woman with dreams and desires. No one needed to know. Tomorrow she would pick up the pieces again and press back into that life of care.

The ride into the foothills was blissful torture for Will. His senses, heightened by the physical contact with the woman in front of him, were sharp. He could smell her hair, a mixture of some sweet soap, smoke, and sunlight. He delighted in her nearness, but dreaded the outcome of their time together. If spending the night in a cave with the boss's daughter wasn't enough for him to get the sack, then riding along with his arms wrapped around her possessively was sure to do the trick.

The steady, swish, swish of his jeans against her back side was just about to force him to start walking when Katie raised a small hand and pointed to a cabin nestled in the woods. He turned Whisper toward it and kicked the tired animal into a quick jog.

As he approached, a young man rode a spotted pony from the trees. The boy couldn't have been more than thirteen, but his dark eyes were cautious. He wore no shirt, just leather breeches and tall moccasins. His skin was bronzed by the sun and his long black hair hung loose behind him. For a moment Will's hand hovered over the pistol on his hip, but then the boy waved and smiled, spurring his horse toward them.

"Sean!" Katie yelled excitedly, waving her hand. Soon the boy was beside them and with a big grin reached a hand out to Katie.

"Well, cousin," he said, "I see you finally made it." His eyes turned to Will questioningly.

Together they rode to the cabin where a woman, a squaw, stood with a girl of about eleven. Will looked at the woman, the child and then the boy, recognizing them as a family. Before they'd come to a complete stop, Katie threw her leg over Whisper's neck and slid to the ground. She raced up the stairs, grasping the woman and then the girl in a tight hug.

Where's Uncle Brion?" she asked. "How is he? We had a terrible time getting here. Oh dear."

She suddenly whirled looking at Will for the first time and bright spots of red spread across her cheeks. "Um. This is Will. He's Pa's new foreman. Never mind though." She took the woman's hand, and pulling her along with her, entered the cabin. Will just caught the small woman turning her braid-bedecked head toward him for a moment, a sly grin spreading across her face.

"You might as well swing down, too," Sean said, sliding off his pony and reaching for the bridle reins. "You go on in and see Da' and I'll see to your horse."

Will smiled and climbed down, giving Whisper a sound pat on the neck as he walked up the stairs and across the porch.

Once inside the simple but homey cabin, Will saw Katie sitting next to a cot by a large stone fireplace. On the pallet, next to the fire, lay a man with hair as red as his roan's mane, and just as mixed with white. He was holding Katie's hand and looking at her fondly, asking her questions in a voice thick with an Irish brogue.

"Sean, boy," he called across the room as his son came through the door. "You'll need to round up the ponies for these two. I'm pretty sure they'll be needing them." He turned his eyes back to his niece. "Now me darlin' little Kat, tell me what happened."

As Katie recounted the events of the previous day and night, her uncle's eyes kept straying to Will, who stood twisting his old hat in his hands.

"I see," the older man said sharply. "Well, you're safe and sound now and that's all what matters." He patted Katie's hand and smiled. "Wynonna, why don't you put some of that cornbread on the table for you and Katie while I have a little talk with this young man."

Will watched in trepidation as Katie rose and walked to the big table on the other side of the room. He watched as the amber haired-girl hugged her raven-haired aunt again and settled down for a chat, before he stepped toward what could only be his day of reckoning.

"You did well, laddie," Brion Blakely said without preamble. "You brought the two of you through a bad time, and safely, too. I'd say that's something."

Will let out a breath he hadn't realized he was holding, his whole body sagging with relief that he wasn't to be berated for his time alone with Katie.

"Now tell me a little about yourself," Brion said, a soft twinkle in his eye.

Across the room Katie sat at the table with her aunt. It had been a surprise to her whole family when Brion had married the Indian woman, but it was evident that he'd done it for love. Wynonna, Winny to her family, was a strange sort and not truly what one would expect of one of her race. She had been raised in a mission for most of her life and was a Catholic through and through, though you'd never be able to tell by her traditional dress and looks. Usually a reserved woman, when roused she was a force to be reckoned with, and her sheer determination had probably saved her whole family a time or two. At the moment, her steely gaze was fixed on her niece's face and Katie found herself squirming like a child caught with his hand in the cookie jar.

"He is very handsome. No?" Winny tilted her head toward the young man still speaking in low tones to her husband. Katie felt a warm blush creep across her face.

"Aunt Winny, that is completely irrelevant. What matters is if he can ease some of the work from Pa and Uncle Benji."

"Pah!" Winny's face grimaced. "He is young. You marry him."

Katie gasped, desperately hoping that the men hadn't heard. "Aunt Winny!" She kept her voice to a shocked whisper. "I'm far too old to think of marriage now.

Besides, Mr. Robertson has come here as a foreman. He probably has a sweetheart he'll send for as soon as he can."

Katie's aunt waved her hand dismissively, then with a smirk she lifted her voice. "You. Young man. How old you are?"

Will's head snapped around as the question obviously directed at him rang out. "Twenty-eight, ma'am," he replied politely.

"You have sweetheart back home?" Winny went on persistently.

"Uh, No ma'am." Will felt even more confused and flustered by the minute.

"Good," the petite woman called back. "You marry our pretty Kat, then," she said cheerfully, nodding her head just once as if to punctuate her statement.

Silence fell like a lead weight across the whole cabin as Will's startled eyes met Katie's wide, shocked ones. The silence crept along the walls and ceiling of the entire cabin, filling it with an icy chill. Then suddenly the whole thing shattered at the loud guffaw coming from the cot by the fire place. Will looked in wonderment as the burly form of Brion Blakely doubled over in laughter. The man had tears streaming down his cheeks as he pointed at first Will, then at Katie.

His wife on the other hand stood to her full, all be it minimal, height placing her hands on her hips. "Why you laugh, Bri-one?" she asked tersely. "They have spent a night in the wilds already, they should just marry." Again she nodded as if to put paid to the whole discussion as her husband struggled to gain control of himself.

Will's eyes never left Katie's face, which was now completely crimson. He could feel his own ears flaming, but still he just stood there like a pole-axed steer, staring.

"Now wife," Brion's chortling voice echoed through the room. "You leave these two young people alone. There's no harm done and I'm sure that Josh'll understand." He chuckled again, but noticed as his wife shook her head in disgust then launched into a tirade in her native language, now glaring at him.

"You youngin's better go on outside," he whispered low to Will, indicating the door with a jerk of his chin. "Let her wind down a bit, then we'll have some real grub."

Jamming his hat onto his head, Will strode toward Katie and offered her his arm, which she took reluctantly and together they walked out onto the front stoop.

"I'm… I'm…Oh, I'm so sorry, Mr. Robertson," Katie stammered.

Will smiled down at her. "It's alright. No harm done," he replied, still not relinquishing her arm from his.

The sound of galloping feet pulled Will and Katie from their own silent thoughts, and they watched as young Sean drove a group of about eight ponies into a rail corral. He then wheeled his own mount and rode to greet them.

"I've brought the stock in," he stated without preamble. "We can go get your gear whenever you're ready, or you can tell me where to go and I'll bring it back."

Finally relinquishing the warm hand tucked in at his elbow, Will replied, "No, I'll go with you. That will give Ms. Katie a chance to catch up with your folks." And with that he walked toward the corral to pick a mount.

Katie sighed. She knew she hadn't heard the last of her aunt's ideas on matrimony, but there was no way to leave yet. With a deep sigh she turned back to the cabin door. She had just lifted the latch, prepared to enter, when a small hand slipped into hers and she turned to look into the face of her little cousin.

"Well, now where have you been?" she asked.

"I just went for a walk to let you grownups have some time to chat," the girl replied in a matter of fact way.

Katie smiled and pulled the young girl to her. "We don't see enough of you at the ranch lately, Annabelle. You need to talk that grumpy old man into bringing you down more often."

The girl shrugged in reply. "We would have come a couple of weeks ago, but Pa hurt his leg, so me and Sean have been keeping up with everything. I figured we'd get down eventually this summer. That's why when Running-Deer stopped by, Pa asked him to let your pa know we could use some supplies."

Katie smiled. "You are too grown up for your age," she told the girl, studying her lovely face. Annabelle would be a beauty someday. Her small heart-shaped face with smooth, straight features was lovely already. Large dark brown, inquisitive eyes, were soft and intelligent. Her black hair hung in two braids over her shoulders while a rose-bud mouth smiled up at Katie.

"How's that different from you?" the girl asked in practical innocence, then opened the door to her home and walked in.

Although the words were not meant with malice, they struck deep in Katie's heart.

Will swung up on the little pinto mustang and picked up the lead rope of another horse while Sean did the same, and together they headed back toward the cave that he and Katie had left just that morning. He looked around him as he headed back toward the east, noting the snug home, the low log barn for the horses, and the well-tended kitchen garden. Brion Blakely had a fine place here, but not just that he had a home.

Will had all but forgotten what home was. His father had died in the War Between the States, leaving his mother with nothing but two small boys to raise. When she was gone he had just started drifting. Home. The word resonated through him until he vibrated like a plucked guitar string. Well, maybe if he just played his cards right, and maybe, if Mr. James didn't run him off the ranch for being out all night with his daughter, he could still have some type of home. He could ride for the brand until he earned a piece of the ranch, then maybe build himself a little cabin, a place to call home.

He could almost picture it in his mind's eye. A few head of cattle, a string of horses. A tidy little house with Katie standing at the door. The vision startled him so much that he pulled his pony up short and just sat there in shock until Sean's intense stare snapped him back to his senses.

"You alright Mr.?" the boy finally asked as they stood in the middle of the trail.

"Oh, sorry," Will said abashedly. "Just wool-gathering, I guess." He kicked his heels to his pony and led the way on toward the cave.

Will set his jaw, determined to put the image of the honey-haired woman from his mind, but no matter how hard he tried, he couldn't shake the vision. Why in the world would he have imagined his place like that? True enough, Katie was a beautiful woman. She was smart, determined and never flinched from hard work, but she was also the cattleman's daughter, which meant she was off limits. Maybe someday he'd have time for a real home, perhaps even a family. The sudden longing that rose in his heart stopped him from breathing as loneliness settled into his soul like a poison.

It took less time to reach the cave than Will expected. Sean knew these hills well and soon they found themselves settling nervous horses as they approached the carcass of the bear. By now the meat would have spoiled, but Sean quickly skinned it while Will loaded up the pack horses.

"Ma'll sure like having this," Sean chimed as he tied the pelt in a bundle.

It didn't take long for Will and Sean to return to the cabin. The boy knew a short-cut over rough country that brought them back well before sun down, and they made good time by keeping their mounts to a steady trot. By the time they returned, supper was cooking and for the most part an amiable peace had settled over the cozy cabin.

Katie sat doing mending with her young cousin while Winny was busy in the kitchen. Brion lay reading a book with his bandaged leg propped up on pillows. The domestic scene twisted Will's gut with longing.

"You wash up for dinner," Winny said abruptly as the two riders stepped into the house. "We eat soon." She gave Will a knowing grin, then began placing items on the table.

Dinner was delicious. A haunch of fresh venison roasted and tender, with vegetables browned in fat and liberally seasoned with herbs and salt. There was even a cake for desert.

"You too skinny," Winny scolded Will, pointing her fork like a scepter. "You need to fatten him up," she said to Katie, now pointing the definitive fork at her.

"Aunt Winny, what do I have to do with it?" Katie protested.

"Pah," Winny snorted. "You see him eat. He is starved. You feed him."

Katie groaned and shook her head.

"I'm eating so much because I missed breakfast and lunch," Will proclaimed, trying to intercede for Katie. "And this is just about the best grub I've tasted in a long time," he added for good measure.

Again Winny waved her fork at him, but this time with a smile. "You still too skinny." She flashed an accusing look at Katie, who was studying her plate with intent purpose.

"Ma'am, I swear they feed me plenty down at the Broken J…" Will began to protest again, but was interrupted by Brion's freckled hand on his arm.

"Give over son," the older man said with a smile. "Once my Wynonna gets an idea in her head, no one will ever shift it save the good Lord himself."

That night Will bunked down with Sean in a room that had been added to the back of the cabin, while Katie shared with her young cousin Annabelle, in the room across the hall. For what seemed like hours Will tossed on the small bunk, but sleep would not come. Instead, he kept thinking of the beautiful young woman sleeping only feet away, and his heart thundered in his ears.

Katie might be only a few feet away across a narrow hall, but to him she was as inaccessible as if she lived a world away. She was the boss's daughter and he rode for the brand; it could never be. With a deep sigh, he rolled over facing the wall and tried to sleep.

Katie lay awake in the darkness studying the shadows of the rafters overhead. The soft sound of her cousin's steady breathing only emphasized the fact the she herself could not sleep.

Across the hall Will slept. Why couldn't she get him out of her mind? Closing her eyes, she could picture his face. His clear eyes and dark wavy hair. His smile when something pleased him. She felt again the thrill of his hand around her waist and the press of his body at her back as they rode the day before. She should never have given in to her desire to be cared for. It was impossible. She would just have to put him out of her mind. She had work to do and no time for a man in her life. That dream was past. Heaving a deep sigh, Katie rolled to her side, staring at the wall and willed herself to sleep.

The next morning broke clear and bright without a cloud in the sky. Immediately after breakfast, Katie and Will mounted up and bid their farewells to her uncle and his family. Her aunt had been very quiet during the morning meal, which surprised Katie until just before they left.

"Mr. Robertson," Winny called as they sat their horses in the yard. "You take care of our Kat. She is for you." Before anyone could say another word, she turned and walked back into the cabin.

"You two get on now," was all Brion said, and waved them out of the yard with a chuckle.

It was a long, quiet ride back down the mountain and homeward. Each of them seemed to be drawn deeper and deeper into their own thoughts.

Will found himself longing for Katie to speak to him, to point out things of importance as they rode along, but she was as wrapped up in her own world as he was, and silently they plodded on. They ate in their saddles, nibbling the cold venison sandwiches Winny had packed for them, sneaking quick glimpses at each other now and then.

Katie noticed the dark stubble on Will's jaw and the drawn, tired lines around his eyes. Will could see dark circles under Katie's eyes and knew what a toll this trip had taken on her. Reaching the relatively flat land of the prairie, they pushed their horses into an easy canter, the steady four-four beat of the horse's hooves keeping time with the sun's slow descent.

All around, bright colors of the prairie sparkled after the cleansing showers from the day before. Here and there small pools of water dotted tiny gullies and sparkled like jewels in the afternoon sun. The sun had just passed its apex when they spotted two riders headed their way. Will eased his rifle in its scabbard, but soon recognized Isadoro and the blacksmith Deeks as they galloped toward them on lathered horses.

"Who Whee!" Deeks called. "We been plumb worried sick 'bout you two youngin's," he said, pulling his horse up in front of them. The old man's face was split into a wide grin as he hunched over his saddle, letting his horse breath.

"I ain't been out in these parts in ages and you two done just about broke this ol' back o' mine. But that's no matter, what's important is you're alright. Ya' are ain't ya?" he added, eyeing them with concern.

"They're fine," Isadoro chided. "But I think they have a good deal of explaining to do on the way home." His dark eyes narrowed on Will, then turned to Katie.

"Grans, we're fine but it is a long story. Let's get moving and I'll tell you all about it, I just want to get home. First though tell me, did the herd get off alright? Was there any trouble? When did they go?"

Isadore swung his gray horse toward home, shaking his head at his granddaughter's questions. She would never change, this one, always thinking of everyone else, always worried about the ranch. Frustration made his words come out sharper than he had intended.

"Everything went just fine and the herd is well on its way to Casper. The world won't end just because you're not there to tell people what to do, you know. Now you tell me what happened to you. Bianca is beside herself with worry. When your horses came back without you, I thought she'd saddle up and head out herself." His dark words fell like a shroud on Katie and she cast a quick glance at Will.

"We didn't mean to worry anyone," he stated, his words clipped. "I'm sure you'll understand when Ms. James explains," he ended, his lips compressed into a grim line.

Chapter 8

Katie stomped into her boots, using her frustration and anger to slam them onto her feet. For the past four days she had been working around the ranch, just waiting for her father and the rest of the men to return to the ranch.

She had been furious when she'd been informed that the other girls had all gone along and that her father had left word that she was not to try to catch them up. She'd argued, and ranted, and even stamped her booted foot a few times in pure temper but her grandfather had stood firm as had Nona, Chen Lou and anyone else who was left on the ranch.

It was Isadoro's soft voice that had finally put paid to the issue though. Grans wasn't a tall man, but within him there was a presence, energy, and intelligence that could match any of the larger men on the ranch. He'd looked at her, his cinnamon eyes soft but firm.

"You're staying here," he said bluntly. "There is no use in you two charging off after a herd that has already been on the trail for three days. Your pa and the others are old hands and they know what to do. Be still." He'd then turned and walked away, leaving no doubt he expected her to heed his words.

Katie stood from her bed where she'd settled to pull her boots on and sighed. He was right and she knew it. The crew that had gone with her father was more than big enough to get them to Casper safely. It just rubbed the wrong way that she wasn't along. Trying to look on the bright side of it all, she could at least grudgingly be happy for her sisters and the fact that they would have a chance to go to town, something that happened rarely at best.

Again huffing a deep sigh, she stepped out of her room and headed to breakfast. She knew her grandfather would have a list of chores and odd jobs to be done today, just like he had done for nearly a week. She and Will had both been given assignments, and she was determined to see them through before the rest of her family returned. This was her home, and it deserved her undivided attention.

Will threw himself back into the work on the ranch with a vengeance. Isadore had stepped in to see that things were done while Joshua and the rest of the men were gone, and his energy was contagious. Each day at breakfast the aging builder would go over the work for the day, and all the men would listen intently, heading out to their assigned jobs.

Will had volunteered several times to check the herd or ride the few fence lines, trying to get away from the ranch and specifically an attractive young woman, but each day he found his chores kept him close to the house. More than once he wondered if Katie's grandfather did it on purpose to keep an eye on him, but he quickly put those thoughts away.

Today he was working with the blacksmith Deeks, helping to stoke the fire to heat the new horseshoes being formed by the thick-set man. Deeks had been a blacksmith his whole life and it showed in the muscles of his arms and chest, but he was now stooped with age, and after years of bearing the weight of horses as he'd shoed them, he seemed to be in almost constant pain. Today Will's job was to assist him in shoeing what was left of the remuda. He stoked the fire, and one by one brought the horses to the older man. The day was hot and before noon both men had stripped their shirts in the sweltering heat of the forge.

Will hadn't seen Katie all day, and although he'd worked with her off and on over the past few days, he suddenly realized that he'd had little time with her at all. Again he wondered if this was Isadoro's plan and he couldn't blame the man for his protectiveness, if that's what it was, especially considering the circumstances of their recent trip to the Wind River Range. With a shiver, he wondered if his time at the Broken J was limited to the day that Joshua James rode back onto the ranch.

Working the billows of the forge, urging the fire to a red hot glow and completely engrossed in his thoughts, he didn't notice as Katie rode up with a few more horses in tow. He looked up just as she stepped from her saddle and for a long moment their eyes met. Will's heart picked up its pace and he couldn't drag his gaze from her face. Her green eyes sparkled and soft color, painted by the rays of the afternoon sun, graced her cheeks. Time seemed to freeze as they stood staring at each other. The sound of Deeks' hammer ringing out on his anvil snapped them from their stupor.

"Katie, you tie them horses over there," Deeks said, pointing with the large hammer in his blackened hand. "I reckon they're the last ones for today." The old black smith's voice crackled like his fire.

Katie dragged her eyes away from Will Robertson, who stood under the low-roofed shed. His lean body rippled with muscles as he held the handles of the billows, the warm glow of the coals casting each angle in relief as sweat ran in droplets along his chest and over his flat stomach. She found her mouth had gone suddenly dry.

"Katie!" Deeks' voice echoed again and she snatched her eyes away from the younger man, a deep blush rising along her cheeks. "Get them horses tied and head in to see if Bianca needs you." The blacksmiths words were sharp, demanding, leaving no room for argument.

In slow, jerky motions the girl did as she was told. Will watched her as she secured the horses to the hitching rail, then turning on her small, booted heel and walked toward the house.

Quite suddenly Will breathed again. He'd been standing there looking at her, looking at him, and his breath had just left his body, without warning, as he'd stood rooted to the spot by her heady green gaze.

Chapter 9

Casper Wyoming   August, 1888.

Joshua James stepped out of the bank and headed for the post office. The cattle had been sold and loaded on the train, and his job was done. He'd deposited the money for the ranch and now turned toward the post office, anticipation making his heart beat loudly.

As he crossed the street, he noticed Benji standing on the train depot platform talking, animatedly, to a well-rounded dark-haired woman in a deep plum colored dress. He shook his head wondering what that could be about, then turned back toward his goal.

As he reached for the door of the post office, a burly black-haired man with sparkling eyes pulled it open, ushering his tall blonde wife out onto the boardwalk with a grin. The woman, finally noticing him as she chatted to her husband, greeted him with a smile and waited for her stocky husband to offer his arm once he was out the door, never once stopping her verbal train of thought.

He smiled again as he watched the couple walk down the street, the quiet man letting his wife ramble on without breaking stride. He missed that companionship, that sense of intimacy that came from just being together, even when there was nothing of importance to discuss. He'd been more than blessed in his life with love, and now just prayed that somehow the good Lord would grant the same for his daughters.

With a sigh he pulled his thoughts back to the task at hand and stepped into the cool dark interior of the post office. There was both a post office and a telegraph office in Casper, and he hoped that either one or the other would have good news for him. He was trying to be patient, but as he grew older, he found that virtue less and less appealing.

He was delighted when the clerk at the counter smiled and handed him a white envelope addressed to him in neat, precise lettering. It was post marked from Illinois, and his spirits lifted with both hope and desire. Taking the envelope and tucking it safely into his pocket, he posted the mail he and the men had prepared, then turned to leave. His palms itched to open the missive he'd received, but he resisted the urge.

"First things first," he reminded himself as he stepped back into the sunny street. There would be time for that later. He only wished he'd had more to report to his brother, Jeremiah.

"I'd better go track down my daughters," he said out loud as he stepped out onto the boardwalk and headed toward the boarding house.

Katie paced the floor of her room, worrying her lower lip between her teeth. There was no question that she found Will Roberston attractive, that she was just plain attracted to him. She'd done her best to stay clear of him, but again and again she found herself in his vicinity. Every morning she would get her list of things to do, choosing each job that would keep her as far from the new foreman as was possible, but by the end of the day the jobs had brought them back together.

She made the circuit of her room again, trying to figure out what to do. Despite the incident in the mountains, it didn't look like Will would be moving on anytime soon. Their time together had proven to her that he was dedicated to the work on the ranch, and she knew he was fascinated with the arrangement on the Broken J that allowed all of those who worked the range to own a share. Of course, once her father returned and heard of their whole adventure, Will's time on the ranch might come to an abrupt end.

For some reason, the dark thought made Katie's breath catch in her lungs. Stopping her pacing, she walked to the window and pushed the heavy curtains aside, looking down on the barn and the smith's shop beside it. She couldn't see anything beneath the low roof, but she remembered all too well the way Will had looked, shirtless by the forge. The bright glow of the embers had cast a rosy hue on his bare torso, the sheen of sweat making him glow in the dim light of the forge. Katie shivered. If she could have ever had a chance at marriage, she would have wished for a man as handsome as the cow puncher. Shaking her head, she turned away from the window.

"Enough day dreaming," she commanded. There was work to be done. Perhaps tomorrow she'd be able to convince Nona that she should stay in and help around the house; that would keep her away from the distraction that was Wilson Robertson. She wondered if Nona would think she was ill or that something was wrong. Katie didn't mind house work, or even cooking, as a matter of fact she made a darn fine cherry pie; she just preferred working outside if she had a choice. She would talk to Nona after dinner, she decided, then went to fix her hair and put on a clean dress.

When Will came in for dinner, he was surprised to find Katie sitting by herself at the table. She looked fresh in a dress of deep russet gingham covered in tiny pink and white flowers. Her face, lightly kissed by the sun, glowed with health and the streaks of gold in her hair glistened in the early evening sunset. For a moment, he let her appearance wash over him, drinking in her loveliness, as he stood and openly stared.

"Oh, good, we are all here now," Nona's voice erupted from behind the screen door. Will looked around, wondering who 'all' could possibly mean, then Isadoro and the other few hands who were still on the ranch walked out of the kitchen door, each carrying a dish.

Soon everyone was seated around the table, grace had been said, and eating commenced. Will had never worked anywhere where all of the hands ate with the family, but over the past few weeks he'd come to understand that here on the Broken J, every hand was family, each member contributing their special part to the success of the whole.

A strange sadness suddenly overwhelmed him as he looked around him at the men and women talking and joking. Isadoro was asking about the accomplishments of the day, while Nona insured that each and every person at the table had more than enough to eat. Will couldn't remember ever feeling so lonely. He'd just put his fork down when Katie looked up from her plate.

"Is everything alright?" she asked quietly, her voice pitched for his ears alone. A wan smile crossed his face.

"I was just thinking what a fine home you have here," he replied, his voice still somber.

"It is pretty amazing," she responded with pride. "It's a little lonely right now, though, with so many people away."

"You must be missing your sisters by now," Will said, realizing that Katie too must feel at least a little lonely.

"I have to confess that at first it was lovely. Everything was so quiet, no one just walking into my room whenever they wanted to talk, or borrowing my things without permission."

Will smiled. "It's nice that you're close to your sisters."

"Do you have family?" Katie asked, still sensing his melancholy mood and wanting to ease it somehow.

"No, ma'am. My family's been gone for a long time now."

He watched as Katie's hand began to reach toward his, an instinctive move to comfort him, then it halted its path and retreated back across the table again. His heart skipped a beat at the gesture of kindness, chasing his dark mood away.

Dinner finished with the usual flurry of noise and jokes, then the men excused themselves and headed back to the bunk house for the night.

Will's job the next day was one of those mundane jobs that required a bit of muscle but almost no mental engagement, and he found his mind wandering as he mucked stalls. He was thinking of home and family, wondering if the dream could ever become a reality.

The horses had been turned out into the large corral, and now each stall required a systematic cleaning. The rhythmic motion of shifting the pitch fork into the straw and refuse, then swinging it into the barrow behind him was so familiar that it seemed to suspend him from his own body.

A light tread on the boards upstairs finally brought him back to his senses, and he cocked his head to hear a little better. A woman's soft voice could be heard grumbling something from the loft, and he shifted himself to just below the hay shoot to see who was up there. He caught a glimpse of Katie as she stepped quickly through the golden hay in the loft, arms outstretched and making soft shooing sounds under her breath. He could also hear a soft clucking noise above, and wondered if somehow one of the chickens had escaped the hen house.

He stepped back a little, trying to see. Suddenly, with a loud squawk a white hen flew straight at the young woman. Katie started, then in what seemed like slow motion, began pinwheeling her arms as she lost her balance and pitched backward into the open hay shoot. Will leapt forward just as Katie plunged toward the small stack of hay on the barn floor, grabbing her and slowing her momentum, which carried them both into the soft heap of bedding.

Katie, still stunned, struggled to get up until Will's laughter engulfed her. Katie stopped trying to rise, her arms and legs tangled with her would-be hero, and began to laugh. Waves of mirth filled the barn as the absurdity of the situation rolled over them. Slowly their laughter quieted. Katie turned her head slightly toward the man beside her in the straw. She was still smiling and her eyes danced.

Will gazed down into her soft lovely face, his smile sliding away as their eyes met just inches from each other.

His head tilted, and as silence fell his lips descended on hers and lingered for an impossible moment. Breaking the kiss, he gazed into her stunned eyes, then both of them seemed to come to their senses. Will jumped to his feet and reached down a hand to help her up.

"You alright ma'am?" he asked, his voice shaky.

"I…" her large, luminous eyes gazed at him. "Oh." Her small white hand covered her mouth for just a moment. Will's face burned with the knowledge that he'd stolen a kiss he had no right to.

Then Katie seemed to get a hold of herself. "Oh, yes, yes. I'm fine," she answered quickly. "Those darn chickens. Someone must have left the coop open this morning. I'd already found the other two and put them back in the fence, but this one was just being difficult."

Will couldn't help but chuckle at the understatement. "Well, as long as you're alright then," he said seriously, looking her up and down. He noticed how the color on her cheeks darkened even as she lowered her eyes from his.

"I supposed I'd better go and fetch her now," Katie stated flatly and turning, walked away.

Will returned to his task, but this time the steady rhythm of his work only forced him to relive, again and again, that little kiss.

Will didn't see Katie for the rest of the day. She'd returned to the loft, aggressively secured the chicken, and headed back to the house. He wondered if she had told anyone about the kiss and his heart sank with the notion. Of course if she had, he probably would be on his way by now, so he hoped for the best.

By supper time he was feeling more confident. Isadoro hadn't come for him and he'd finished his job, tossing fresh straw into each stall, making it ready for its next occupant. He had just hung his pitch fork on its hook when Deeks came in. "You ready, son?" he called cheerfully. "It's Saturday, ya know."

Will shook his head. Saturday. He'd completely forgotten, but he quickly followed Deeks to the bath house. This was another one of those features that had astounded him about the ranch. They built a whole bath house with three large copper tubs right next to the bunk house. There was a large cook stove for heating water, and the room had its own tall, handled pump. In reality, it was an ingenious way to provide this needed feature for the hands. With the large number of men on the ranch it served two purposes. Not only was it a convenient way to maintain cleanliness, it also insured that the pump wouldn't freeze up come winter.

Tonight was special, though. With only Deeks, Isadore and Will working the ranch, they each had a full tub and didn't have to hurry to ensure that the next man in line had hot water. It would feel good to wash the week's grit and grime from his weary body, and in no time he was lounging in the hot water, letting it work the kinks out of the tense muscles in his neck and shoulders.

Will knew he'd never have a place as fine as the one that Joshua James and his men had created, but in his heart he determined to have a home of his own someday. Will leaned back, letting his head rest on the high back of the big tub, and closed his eyes. The voices of the other two men talking about the labors of the day were a soft buzzing in his ears, and in moments Will had drifted off to sleep;

bright green eyes and a pretty mouth smiled up at him from his dreams.

Will woke with a snort and a shout as a bucket of water descended over him. With a howl, he raised himself from the tepid water and glared at the two older men who had, like juveniles, doused him. Grabbing a towel, he wrapped it around himself and disgruntledly stepped onto the plank floor, while the other two held on to each other to keep from falling over with laughter.

Will dressed, feeling grumpy, while recognizing that the joke on him was a good one. He'd let his guard down and paid for it, but more than that, he was irritated that he'd dreamed of Katie. He had to put her out of his head. He had to hang on to this job long enough to get what he wanted.

The other men had already headed to the house by the time he finished dressing, stalked out of the bath house, and trudged wearily to the back porch. It was obvious from the start that tonight something was different. The table was spread with a bright table cloth and everything had been set out precisely. With only six people left on the ranch only one table was needed and someone had gone to the trouble of making everything look especially nice.

Will joined the other men at the table as the women carried the last dishes out. Nona Bianca was smiling radiantly as she piped up and said, "I want you all to know that Katie did all of the cooking tonight."

Dinner was different than anything that Will could ever remember eating. A heavy bowl full of hard boiled eggs in a rich creamy sauce, liberally seasoned with salt and pepper was the main course and was served with crisp, browned potatoes, cut into little cubes. There were loaves of fresh bread and a fresh salad of cucumber and tomato in a sweet vinegar dressing. It was simple, fair, but hearty and filling as well as tasty.

"That was a wonderful meal, Katie," Isadoro stated, wiping his mouth with a bright napkin. "It's been too long since you did any real cooking." Katie smiled at her grandfather, and when the other men added their praise, she waved them away, embarrassed by all of the fuss.

"That's not the best part, yet," Nona said, rising from the table. "Now we have pie. Come Katie, you help me." And together the two woman rose and walked back into the kitchen. Chen Lou leaned back in his chair at the table and gave a contented burp.

The cherry pie was just about the best Will had ever eaten and he told Katie so. He smiled when shy color rose in her cheeks, but was careful not to be too forward. It wouldn't do to get run off of the ranch at this point.

For the next two days, Will was kept busier than ever doing odd jobs around the ranch. It seemed like the one that most often fell to him was chopping wood, and soon he'd stacked what he thought must surely be enough to last three winters. He had just finished carrying a load into the kitchen and was stacking it in the wood box when the sound of horses approaching caught his ear.

Standing, he strode through the house and out onto the porch just in time to see the ranch hands peel away from the chuck wagon and another heavy freight wagon. The sound of running feet announced Katie's arrival as she raced down the stairs and outside to greet the wagons.

"Pa!" She called excitedly, then froze as she saw not her Pa on the wagon seat, but Benji, and next to him, a pretty buxom woman in a lovely purple gown. Katie gaped as Benji pushed his hat back on his head, sitting high up on the wagon seat, boot propped on the rails.

"Hello, darling." His deep voice was full of humor. "I wanted to be the first to introduce you to my lovely wife, Cathleen," he said with a smile.

Katie's jaw dropped, but soon a smile spread across her delicate features. "Hello," she finally managed, just as her father rode up. He smiled softly at his oldest daughter and swung down from his mount. Katie raced into his arms, all annoyance at him leaving without her wiped away by the relief that he and the rest of the family had returned safely.

Joshua wrapped his arms around his girl and held her tight, thankful that she'd returned safely to him. Raising his head slightly, his icy blue gaze drove straight toward Will, whose whole being froze for just a moment, until the old man, ever so slightly, nodded his head.

Will began breathing again. It looked like the boss might not throw him out just yet. A strange feeling came over Will, a quietness mixed with longing.

No sooner had Will recognized the feeling of respect and admiration growing inside of him, then loud squeals pierced the quiet and the five other James girls came tumbling out of the wagons, racing toward Katie with excited calls, washing her away and into the house on a wave of laughter.

Will watched as Benji climbed down from the wagon, a bright smile lighting his rugged face as he walked around to the other side and helped his new wife down. Even from where he stood on the porch, Will could see the admiration on Benji's face as he looked at the woman. She was by no means what could be called a tiny girl. She was mature and her figure was full of well-rounded curves, but by the look on the foreman's face, he was completely smitten.

Joshua James stomped his way up the stairs to the porch, and stretched out a hand to the young man standing there.

"Thank you for bringing my Kate back to us safely son," the older man said gently. "I'd like to hear all about that very soon," he added with a significant look. "For now, how about you help get the stock settled, then come into the house for some coffee and we'll talk."

"Yes, sir," Will replied, his heart thumping in his chest with relief, then stepped out into the yard.

Behind him, he heard the screen door slam and the excited ramblings of Bianca Lioné as she raced from the house, spouting joyous words of English and Italian that were so jumbled he didn't think anyone could make heads nor tails of them. Looking over his shoulder, he heard the wind being knocked out of Benji's new bride as the other woman grasped her in a crushing hug. Will couldn't help but smile. Did the dark-haired woman have any idea what she had signed on for by marrying Benjamin Smith? He wondered as Bianca's voice followed him toward the barn.

"Algori, Algori! Congratulations!" Bianca's sing song voice bounced through the air, as she practically dragged the startled woman into the house.

Will entered the barn and began untacking the horses he'd taken from the weary men in the ranch yard.

He'd told them to go get washed up and have a rest and that he'd catch up on news of the drive later. The men had thankfully handed over their mounts and headed for their abode.

Will was relieved to see that everyone seemed fit, and that although tired from the long trek to Casper and back, both men and horses were none the worse for wear. He wished that he'd been able to go with them, but then thought of the time he'd had with Katie and couldn't find regret among the emotions he was feeling.

"Besides, I'll be there next time," he said confidently.

"You talkin' to yerself now, sonny," a crotchety old voice rasped behind him. Will turned to see the white-haired chuck wagon cook enter the barn leading his team.

"They says that's a sure sign of insanity, ya' know." The old man chuckled, and slapped Will on the shoulder hard enough to make him sway; the skinny, old man still packed a wallop.

"I can put the team up for you if you'd like," Will offered, trying to spare the older man extra work.

"No ya cain't," the other man retorted. "I been tending these two ornery cusses since they come to this ranch, and ain't no one else gonna do it but me still." His withered jaw snapped shut on his toothless mouth with grim determination.

"Alright," Will said, raising his hands in surrender. The old man looked at him with rheumy eyes and grinned.

"What you been doin' while we was off getting' them cows to market, sonny? You can tell old Billy. I knows how to keep a secret." The old eyes twinkled mischievously at Will, who didn't know what to say. "Meybe you got up to some sparkin' while the old man was away. Huh?" Billy added with a wink.

Will gasped, feeling a flush rise up along his neck and over his whole face. His mind raced back to his single unsolicited kiss.

The other man's cackle nearly undid Will. He turned, watching as the old man doubled over laughing his head off and pointing at Will.

"You done shoulda' seen your face," Billy chortled. "You looked as guilty as a pup in a puddle." His laughter shook him again and Will worried the little fella would crack a rib, but then Billy sobered again, looking Will full in the face.

"You young people today. Yer all just too serious. You have all these here blessings right on your door step and ya cain't even see it," Billy huffed, but didn't slow down now that he was warming up. "When I was a young man, I had to fight Injuns and lived in a sod hut. You youngin's these days gots a warm bed ever' night, plenty of food, and an easy life. Why, you don't seem to recognize opportunity when it practically knocks you on the head. There you have a pretty little girl sittin' up in that house, and you won't even give her a howdy do'. No, no, you're all wrapped up in your life and work and can't see the forest for the trees. Well if you asked me…"

"I didn't ask you," Will's voice was soft, but cut off the old man's ramblings just the same.

For a moment Billy's cloudy eyes met Wills bright hazel glare but didn't back down.

"Pah!" he spat. "You go on then, and just do as ya please. Don't listen to a man more'n twice your age and then some. I've lived a bit boy, and I'll speak my mind when I want." With that the old cook led his team to a nearby stall and began disgruntledly stripping the harness.

Feeling guilty, Will walked over and leaned on the stalls railing. "I'm sorry, old-timer," Will said gently.

Billy turned, a scowl still marring his face. Then the twinkle returned to his eyes.

"It's alright sonny, you are the way you are and I can be an old fool sometimes. I reckon what with Benji up and gittin' hisself a mail-order bride... well even an old coot like me can get notions." He smiled his toothless grin again and turned back to his work.

Will unsaddled the horses, giving them a good feed and a rub down while Cookie worked on his team, but the whole time the old man's words pricked him like a burr under his saddle. Billy hadn't meant to upset him; how could the old man know the thoughts that had been haunting him for days. He desperately wanted a home and a woman like Katie would fit right in with his dreams. Under any other circumstances, he would have courted a woman like her for all he was worth but to do so now, here, would bring an end to any dreams that would allow him a chance to offer any woman a home. A deep sigh escaped him as he picked out a hoof, and he was pretty sure he'd heard a chuckle rise from the other side of the barn. The sound did nothing to improve his mood.

Chapter 10

Back in the house, Katie was regaled with the adventures, sights and sounds of the drive by four of her five sisters. Mae, of course, had made a bee-line for her pony. After each girl had a turn recounting some event or item from their trip to Casper, Meg turned to Katie with a dreamy look in her eye.

"Now, Katie you must tell us all about your trip to Uncle Brion's. It must have been so romantic getting caught in the rain with that handsome cowboy," she said, twirling herself onto the bed.

"Romantic!" Katie exclaimed. "We were almost eaten by a bear!" At this pronouncement, Meg jumped up from the bed and all of the sisters gathered around waiting for Katie to tell the tale.

"I thought you said it wasn't romantic." Meg groused giving Katie and evil look. "He rescued you from an evil ol' bear and you don't think that's romantic?"

"Did you really have to ride double?" Fiona spoke up, her quiet voice soft with wonder.

Katie blushed but nodded her head. For some reason the twins put their heads together and giggled.

"It didn't mean anything," Katie reminded them. "What else could we do? We were just being practical."

"Did he put his arms around you?" Issy asked, a sly grin on her face. Katie's blush deepened and the girls collapsed on the bed again in a heap.

"Oh, I want a cowboy to put his arms around me some day," Meg sighed. "He'll be tall, dark and handsome and such a gentleman. I can just imagine it." Her eyes took on a faraway look and they could all tell that was exactly what she was doing.

"Now stop all of this chatter," Katie finally asserted, her voice growing firm. "Mr. Robertson is the foreman here and that's all. He did his best to see that we made it to Uncle Brion safely. So just put all of these silly romantic notions out of your head." Her voice never wavered, but for just a moment she wondered if she was trying to convince her sisters or herself.

Unbidden, the memory of that one kiss in the hay mow washed over her, and her whole body tingled. Her woman's heart longed for the romance Meg went on about so dreamily, but her head told her that was not in the cards for her. She sighed heavily, forgetting her sisters for a moment, only to be reminded of them again as they burst, once more, into a bout of giggles.

"You know, Katie," Alexis spoke, her voice calm as always. "Uncle Benji's a lot older than you and he just got married. You just never know what could happen." She looked meaningfully at her oldest sister, then turned her eyes back toward her twin, sharing a look they reserved for their own secrets.

The sound of Nona's raised voice brought all of the girls to their feet and scrambling for the hall. As they exited Katie's room, they could hear the loud voice of Uncle Benji as he argued with the matron of the house.

"I said we're goin' to the soddy and we're goin'!" Benji shouted. "Now you can either help me or not, it's up to you."

Leaning over the railing of the bent wood railing the girls saw Nona raise her hands in the air in preparation for another tirade but she never had the chance to get started. A strong, weather-browned hand stretched out and gently came to rest on their grandmother's shoulder. She wheeled around, looking into the soft brown eyes of her husband.

"Leave it, Bia," he said gently. "He's a grown man and has a right to his own decisions." Nona's mouth hung open for just a moment before she closed it with a snap, and as quickly as her temper had come up, it was gone.

"Well, Benjamin, if you insist. I was just thinking of your new bride is all. She looks such a lady and to have to stay in the soddy…" Her voice trailed off as she saw the woman of whom she spoke standing slump-shouldered with embarrassment on the front porch.

Nona's face softened, turning a distinctive shade of pink. Then with one nod of her head, she turned and shouted up the stairs for the girls, an all too-familiar tone in her voice. With that tone, the girls scrambled down the stairs to await their marching orders.

In no time a steady stream of furniture, linens and household goods were making their way to the small sod shack in the far corner of the property. Grans Isadoro and the other men had set to tidying the place, and soon the girls were busy cleaning and decorating what had been their first home.

Cathleen, though obviously embarrassed by all of the fuss, accepted the help gratefully and soon had the tiny home serviceable.

"I'm so sorry for being so much trouble," she said, her unassuming voice soft as the girls dusted, swept and hung curtains. "Ben said we'd only be staying her a couple of weeks and I do hate to put you all out."

Katie looked at the soft plump woman and smiled. "You're no trouble at all," she said brightly. "You're family." Then she hugged her new auntie, surprised to see a tear slide down her delicate pale cheek.

Supper that night was a huge affair. As soon as Nona had found out about Benji's new bride, she'd begun cooking. She had chickens roasting in the massive cook stove, with pots of potatoes and carrots boiling softly away on the hob. A gigantic gingerbread cake sat on the work table waiting its turn in the oven, while Chen Lou, madly grumbling in his native tongue, vigorously whipped a large bowl of cream into stiff peaks before adding sugar and whipping some more.

The girls were busy chopping a variety of fresh vegetables and making rolled biscuits to go with the special meal. Even Cookie and the other hands pitched in by spreading brightly colored table clothes over the two huge tables at the back of the house and setting the table.

It was indeed a festive supper that Benji brought his new bride back to. She'd changed out of her plum traveling dress at the soddy, and now wore a simple day dress in a stunning shade of deep red. Benji walked his wife around the table and sat her next to him on the wide bench with a smile, only reluctantly giving up her hand after Joshua James said grace.

The meal was its usual melee with several conversations going on all at one time, but once the large, still-warm gingerbread was carried out to the table, a soft hush fell over them all. Nona, still beaming, placed the cake in front of Benji and Cathleen with a flourish.

"We all want to make you feel welcome here at the Broken J," she said brightly. "I hope you like gingerbread. I just didn't have time to do more."

Cathleen's soft white skin began to flush as she gazed around at the group of people who had all so warmly welcomed her. The rosy blush deepened, creeping up her neck and all the way to the roots of her dark brown hair. It was all too much. She burst into tears, then scrabbled over the bench and raced away. Benji, his eyebrows almost to his hair line, gazed around him in confusion. Shaking his head, he rose and followed after his wife, while a shocked and confused Nona stared bewilderedly about.

"Did I say something wrong?" she finally asked quietly. No one laughed at the obvious chagrin on the older woman's face.

"You didn't do anything wrong, Bianca," Joshua offered kindly. "You know how overwhelming we can all be at the beginning. You just leave her and Benji to get acquainted and I'm sure everything will be just fine."

"Oh," Nona said, suddenly realizing she was still holding the large cake in her hands. She looked at her husband, whose eyes were now glowing up at her.

"Put it down, mi amoré," he said quietly, then lifting his hand, beckoned for her to join him.

Once the cake touched the table the chatter and banter returned as Chen Lou stepped in and began cutting and serving the soft brown confection with liberal amounts of whipped cream on top.

Will found himself chuckling at the evening's events. He remembered how he'd felt when he first arrived at the ranch. It was one of the most confusing places he'd ever been, and it had taken him at least two weeks to learn everyone's names, let alone get over the shock factor of the James' girls working as hands. He could only hope that with a little time, Cathleen would come to see the Broken J as home.

There it was again, that word. Home. His eyes drifted to Katie's across the table and a warmth that had nothing to do with the rays of the setting sun filled him. She was chatting with her sister Meg who was giggling about some comment she'd made. The soft light from the dying sun burnished Katie's hair, causing it to blaze in fiery splendor. The soft blush of her cheeks glowed, and her smile brightened her whole face. She was truly beautiful. The most beautiful woman he'd ever seen.

Will lowered his eyes to his plate, the warmth of a moment ago fading as if whisked away by a winter breeze. The sweet taste of the gingerbread turned to ash in his mouth and his heart twisted within him as he placed his fork on the table, stood, said his good-nights and walked away.

Joshua James studied his daughter as she watched the tall puncher walk away. He could see the affection she felt for the young man glowing in her eyes, and yet he knew just how stubborn his oldest child could be. Silently he whispered a prayer to the Almighty before finishing his cake.

Chapter 11

The work load fell heavily onto Will's shoulders as preparations for the winter ahead began. It was late August and work on the ranch had never been busier. Benji, although still technically the Broken J's primary foreman, began handing things off to Will and spending more and more time near the ranch and his new bride. He'd made it clear that he planned on being out of the soddy and ensconced in his own cabin before the snows came, and he pushed Will and the other men to make sure that they were ready for his retirement when the time came.

Life was a bustle of activity. Cookie, Chen Lou, Nona and others, including the James girls, were busy harvesting the large kitchen garden and preserving and canning food for the long winter ahead. Will and the other hands were cutting and stacking hay in the fields, or piling it in mountainous stacks on large wagons to be hauled back to the barn and hay sheds further out at the ranch. Once the loft above the barn was full, they'd spread more loads out among various sheds and shanties dotting the range to have ready winter fodder on hand if the snows were too bad.

Will drove teams, swung a scythe, stacked, hefted, and hauled hay. He was itchy, sweaty and tired but was pleased with the work getting done. At first he had worried about how the other men would receive him as the ranch foreman, but it was plain after the first day that they had no problem taking orders from a younger man. On the other hand, working side by side with the old hands, and with some judicious advice from Benji and Joshua James, he was learning the ranch in a way he never could have before.

The sun beat down on Will's back as he stood upright on the top of a hay wagon. He stretched tired muscles, leaning on his pitch fork, and scanned the surrounding field. In another day or two the hay would be in and they'd have to scour the surrounding hills, bringing any cattle who had wandered too far from the low prairie down. He felt the warm autumn sun on his bare chest and breathed deeply of the heady smell of freshly mown hay.

One by one he'd been making a mental list of jobs that would need to be completed before the first snow fall, then began adding to that the list of cold weather jobs that would have to be tended. His mind raced as he gazed off toward the far hills. It was a fine land he'd come to, and fleetingly he wondered if he'd ever be able to call a piece of it home. Somehow this wide open range had become a part of him, and the more he rode it, the more he worked it, the more it seeped into his bones. His eyes drifted toward the ranch house in the distance, and his heart gave a lurch as he wondered for just a moment what Katie was doing. Reminding himself that was none of his business, he bent his back once more to the task of stacking hay.

Katie smoothed her soft yellow dress, took a deep breath, and rapped on the door of the little sod shack. Cathleen opened the door with a shy smile and ushered Katie in.

"I just made fresh cookies and thought you might like some," Katie said in greeting, holding out a small plate covered by a cloth.

"That'd be lovely," the other woman said, and directed Katie to the small two-person table by the miniscule cook stove. "Won't you come in for tea?"

"I hope you're settling in alright now," Katie said politely as she placed the cookies on the table and sat herself in a chair.

Cathleen's soft laugh was her initial reply as she placed cups and saucers on the table before pulling a tin of tea off of a shelf. "I won't say it's been easy, but yes, I think I am. It's such a beautiful place and Benjamin says we'll be moving to his own cabin as soon as the snow arrives."

"Oh, I hadn't thought of that," Katie said as she watched Cathleen sit and pour the tea. "Isn't it terribly hard being so far away from everyone, family and friends, I mean?"

"I don't really have any family left," Cathleen said wistfully "and as for friends, I think I'll make my fair share here. I'm learning that life is all about your attitude and not your circumstances."

Katie pondered the other woman's words while she munched a sugar cookie. She found that she truly liked Cathleen and that despite her bumpy start as a member of the Broken J's odd family, she thought that someday they could truly be friends. Cathleen was quiet and reserved, but also had a quick humor hidden just below the surface.

"I don't think I could ever just leave home like you did." Katie began, thinking out loud as she sipped her tea. "I mean my whole family is here and they need me. I've Pa, and all of my sisters, and Nona, Grans, and Yeye Chen Lou aren't getting younger. They need me to look after things."

"I'm proud to see a young woman with a sense of responsibility," Cathleen said, smoothing her skirts and looking across the table at her young guest.

"But what does it really mean to care for your family? Before my father passed…" she paused taking a steadying breath "… he insisted that the only thing that would make him rest easy was to know I was taken care of. It's the biggest reason I decided to become a mail-order bride."

For a moment her eyes took on a faraway look. "Sometimes what we think of as being selfish or self-serving is really what our family wants for us. What they really want is for us to be happy and safe, that's all."

For some reason Cathleen's words made Katie feel uncomfortable. She had always known her place. Her whole life she'd known that as the oldest she had to watch over her family and see that they had everything they needed. Her wants and desires were secondary to theirs. Up until recently, everything she had ever wanted had been right here; she'd been content, happy, satisfied in her role. Why did she feel so restless now? Finishing her tea, she thanked her new aunt for the visit and excused herself. But once she left the cheery confines of the tiny sod shack, she couldn't shake her feeling of unease.

Chapter 12

Brush popping was one of the worst jobs on the ranch and often one of the most dangerous. After the hay had been stored, the hands returned to the mountain passes, working in teams of two and three to push some of the wilder cattle down to the safer winter pastures. Wild-eyed cows with late calves, or small pockets of young cattle hiding out in thickets, gullies and passes, were often just as determined to stay where they were as the men were to see them driven down out of the high ranges.

Will separated the old hands into groups, and with Benji's advice, sent them out to find any animal that had strayed. When Joshua and Katie made it clear that they were on the roster, Will partnered with them and headed for the hills.

They rode quietly, barely speaking and watching for any likely area a steer or cow could be hiding. Katie rode next to her father, with Will to the right of the boss and slightly in the lead. Sometimes he was sure he could feel her eyes on him, but he resisted the urge to look over his shoulder to be sure.

Over the past few weeks he hadn't seen much of Katie and he wondered if she had told anyone about the kiss in the barn. Thinking of it, a warm thrill ran up his spine. The young woman hadn't been cold to him since then; she simply seemed to avoid his company as much as possible.

Will, distracted by his own thoughts, didn't notice Joshua James turn his buckskin toward a clump of bushes along the outskirts of a copse of tall yellow pines. The sound of branches scrapping on leather chaps brought Will back to his task just as the older man pushed an old, mossy horn cow and her puny calf out of the bushes.

Katie, seeing that the cow was about to bolt, spurred her horse toward it, working to squeeze it between herself and her father, forcing the animal to turn toward the lower valley. It was a perfectly reasonable move, but as soon as Will raised his head to study the scene, he could see that the cow had no intentions of being reasonable.

Instead, the red-brindled beast lowered its head, shaking lethal horns six feet wide at a spread that glistened in the bright afternoon sun, as she charged toward Katie's horse. The cow pony began to dodge, but it was obvious that it could never move out of the way fast enough. Whisper responded to the thump of Will's heels in less than a heartbeat, stretching his neck, bearing his teeth and aiming toward the big cow. The beast, seeing the new threat, turned at the last moment, giving just enough room for Katie's pony to escape.

Whisper, still at a dead run, had no time or room to move, but threw his shoulder full into the wild-eyed cow, who, determined to defend her calf, shifted her weight just as the roan horse made impact. Together, the horse, cow and rider tilted, then rolled. Whisper's whole body tumbled, head first, neck beneath shoulders and hind quarters wind-milling as momentum carried the horse through the full summersault.

Will felt himself flying from the saddle as his horse impacted first cow and then earth with a horrifying crack and crash. Stretching his arms in front of him as he soared over the downed body of the cow, Will felt the wrist in his right arm give way as he hit the ground, using his forward motion to roll along his shoulder, and finally coming to a skidding halt on his side. Brambles, grass and brush scrapped and tore at Will's body as it followed along the ground, knocking him senseless for a few moments.

As the darkness around his eyes passed, Will sat up, shaking his head to restore his senses. His arm hurt, but he pushed himself dazedly to a sitting position. The thump of horse's hooves next to him drew his attention and instinctively he lifted his left arm to reach for Whispers reins, but his hand didn't make contact with the roan horse. Instead a small gentle hand grasped his as Katie leapt from her mount and reached for him. He looked up into the shocked and frightened eyes of the girl, still dazed and bewildered.

Slowly another sound penetrated his befuddled mind. The soft huff of a horse, and the sound of a scrabbling animal. Shaking his head to try to clear it, Will followed the sound, taking in the carnage around him.

Off to his right in the distance the big cow hobbled next to her calf, glaring at Joshua's big buckskin helplessly as the cow pony kept her and the calf penned against the trees. Then he saw what was making the soft noises off to his left.

Whisper lay stretched out on his side, head extended in front of him at an odd angle, his hooves making soft twitching motions in the dark earth where he'd fallen. Pushing himself to his knees Will half crawled, half lunged toward his faithful mount, his left hand extending into the animal's red-flecked mane, and stoked the glossy hide.

"Easy, there," he soothed, and the horse nickered low in its throat. "Rest easy now old man." Will's voice broke as the soft, limpid brown eyes turned toward their master's voice and the horse stilled. For long moments,

Will stroked the glossy mane of his most loyal companion, his face pale and his eyes full of pain.

"His neck's broke, son," Joshua's voice was rough with emotion. Will nodded, then once more laid his good hand on Whisper's neck.

"You want me to do it?" Joshua's words were gentle.

Will's voice left him but he shook his head and stood, pulling his pistol awkwardly from its holster. Two small, strong hands took it from him, and he didn't object as Katie cocked the weapon and placed it back into his uninjured hand.

Taking a deep breath to steady himself, Will gripped the heavy revolver and pulled the trigger. The echoing report of the gun's discharge broke his heart and left a hole in his soul.

"He was all I had," his nearly inaudible words fell in the silence after the thunder. Will's knees gave out on him and he sat heavily on the ground, the pistol tumbling from his grasp.

"Not anymore son," Joshua's rugged voice was only just louder than Will's had been. "You're part of this ranch now."

Numb, Will sat on the ground next to the still body of his horse, unable to comprehend the older man's words in his shock.

"Katie," Joshua called, still studying the young man on the ground. "You look after him, while I ride on along and get help."

"Yes, Pa," Katie's' soft voice whispered past Will's ear as she stood by his side. Still looking at her father, she laid a hand on Will's shoulder protectively, then watched as her father galloped away.

Katie stood there, her light hand resting on Will's shoulder, silent tears rolling down her face. Quietly she stepped around his rigid form and knelt, facing the man who sat bewildered on the ground.

"Will." Her voice was gentle, imploring. "Will." He turned weary, grief-stricken eyes toward her. "Will, do you think you can get up on my horse?" His blank eyes pulled at her heart and she reached out to cup a hand along his cheek. He closed his eyes and leaned into her palm.

Katie's soft hand on his cheek seemed to reach deep into Will's soul, and something long forgotten uncoiled, stretched, and broke with in him as tears spilled from his eyes. All of the loss and longing of his life seemed to swell within him like flood waters reaching the top of a dam and pouring over. A ragged breath broke from his lungs and then Katie was holding him. He wrapped his good arm around her waist and buried his head against her as she held him, speaking soothing words, as her tears fell like a blessing on his head.

Katie didn't know how long she stood there holding the cowboy in her arms, feeling his pain. She held him desperately, with a need deeper than any she had ever experienced. This was not the simple loss of a beloved animal, but the loss of a dream, of all dreams.

Bitter tears rolled down her face at the recognition of what it all represented. The loss of things that they had both hoped for, things that could never be. After what seemed like ages, Will pulled himself back together, and she could feel him withdrawing from her in shame at his display of emotion. She wished she had words to tell him that she understood, but they wouldn't come.

She understood that they had both been denied in life what their hearts desired. Not meeting each other's eyes, allowing that strange concession to shared pain, she wrapped his wrist and put it in a sling. Helping him to his feet, she guided him to her horse and half pushed him aboard. He moved stiffly as if his body had forgotten motions that were second nature to him. Once she was sure he wasn't going to fall off, she picked up the reins and began walking back toward the ranch.

Katie had them nearly half way back to the ranch before her father and the other men caught up with them. One of the hands gently took the reins of her horse and another helped her up behind her father on his big gelding. It was a silent ride home.

Katie was exhausted. The danger and emotions of the day had left her drained and bewildered. As soon as she could, she had retreated to her room as Nona and Chen Lou went out to the bunk house to tend Will's wounds.

The last golden rays of the setting sun stretched across her room as she sat on the bed. Her whole body was numb, but within her chest her heart twisted treacherously. She longed to run to the bunk house to check on Will. To hold him in her arms again. He was alone even here among her big, boisterous family, and he'd been alone for a long time. She resonated with an understanding of his need. Her heart screamed for her to go to him to be the one who filled that need in his life, but the whispers of the past haunted her, keeping her rooted to the spot.

A soft knock caused her to lift her head as her father stepped through the door, coming to sit beside her on the bed. "Why are you sitting here in the dark, Katie?" he asked gently.

She looked up at him, studying his glacial blue eyes, but she had no reply.

"That young man is hurting you know," her father said patiently. "Why don't you go to him?"

Katie's eyes grew wide. Was her father saying she should go to Will, comfort him? "You love him, don't you?"

Katie was dumbfounded. How did he know?

"Then why don't you go to him?" This time he waited for her reply.

"I... I can't," she stuttered.

"Why not?" Again the ancient words echoed in her head and fresh tears broke loose and spilled down her pale cheeks.

"I can't Daddy. I have to stay here and take care of you."

Joshua James reached an arm around his daughter's shoulders, a sad smile easing over his craggy features.

"Why Katie? Can't you see that I have everything I need? I have more than enough people to take care of me and your sisters. There's Bianca and Isadoro, Chen Lou and Benji, not to mention all the other men and your sisters. I don't think I could be more well cared for."

"But..." she stuttered again.

"But what?"

"Mama told me I had to take care of you." Her voice quivered. "She said I was the oldest and had to look after all of you."

"Oh, darling." Joshua's voice was soft. Pulling her close, he said gently, "You can't take care of any of us if you can't take care of yourself, and right now you're having such a battle with your heart there won't be anything left of you if you don't let it win. Sometimes listening to your heart is the best way for you to take care of others. Your sisters and I are well cared for, but that young man out there is all alone."

"But I have a responsibility." Katie's words were weak.

"We all have responsibilities, sweetheart, but our first responsibility is to love. God didn't put us on this earth to walk it alone. He put us here to live and to share our lives. His wisdom is higher than ours and if He brings something to you, then that's what you're supposed to have. We can't get through life on our own strength. The only way to have joy is to trust that you have a purpose and that if we believe and accept, life will take us where God wants us to be."

Katie's eyes flew open in wonder as she suddenly understood. Will needed her now, but her family didn't need her to look after them anymore. She wasn't leaving them, just adding a new layer to their already remarkable family. By setting her heart free, she could not only love and protect her family, she could bring someone special to them. Someone who would work alongside her and together build on what her father had started all of those years ago.

Joshua's smile brightened as he saw the truth dawning on his daughter's face. Suddenly, she threw her arms around his neck and kissed his cheek. "I love you Papa," she said, just like she had when she was a little girl.

"I know darlin'. Now I think there's someone else who needs you."

Katie leapt off the bed and dashed down the stairs, her small, booted feet making a thundering racket as she ran.

Will sat propped up in his bed, his arm set and re-hung in its sling. The whole right side of his body was a mass of bruises and scrapes, and his bent and battered heart labored in his chest. Everything he had was gone, and with it all hope had fled.

He eased his leg on the bunk but couldn't find any way to ease his brooding mind. That old cayuse had been the last true possession he had that he could call his own. He was a cowboy without a horse or a home. Within him his heart stuttered, causing his whole chest to feel as if it were wrapped in steel bands. He struggled to breath.

The bunk house door burst open with a loud bang and Katie James stepped into the room. Will groaned. He didn't think his battered heart could take much more. Yet there she stood, the most beautiful woman he'd ever seen, and she might as well have been an ocean away.

He closed his eyes, trying to put her image out of his mind. The sound of booted feet shuffling across the plank floor echoed around him and for a moment he thought she had gone. A darkness passed between him and the lamp on the table, diminishing the soft light that penetrated beneath his eyelids.

The whole bunkhouse was silent and he opened his eyes, only to find Katie standing before him gazing at him with her luminous eyes. His labored breath caught in his throat and for a moment his head spun. How had he come to love her? He'd tried to avoid her, told himself it could never be, and yet somewhere along the way his heart had chosen her. He longed to close his eyes, to shut out her lovely face, to find some dark corner to hide in where he could just forget.

Slowly Katie reached out and drew her hand along the roughened jaw of the injured cowboy, a gentle smile teasing at her lips. Her whole face seemed to glow as she studied his face.

"Will." Her voice was barely audible but plunged deep into his heart. *Not anymore. You're part of this ranch now.* His head suddenly echoed with Joshua's words from a few hours ago. Could it be? Could the old rancher know and approve? Katie smiled as comprehension finally began to dawn on Will's handsome face. She smiled a bright, clear smile that melted his resistance.

Pushing himself to his feet, he looked down at Katie. "You?" His voice failed him.

Katie nodded her head, her eyes declaring the love she felt. And suddenly he understood. Reaching out with his good arm, he pushed a strand of hair away from her face, his work roughened-thumb tracing her jawline in the process. Bright tears sprang to her eyes as a smile spread across his face.

"I didn't mean to fall in love with you." His words were ragged with emotion, as he watched Katie's eyes grow wide with wonder.

"You love me?" she whispered, her eyes glowing.

"From almost the first moment I saw you."

"I love you, too."

This time her words were firm, and his heart sang with the hearing of them. Gently he pulled her to him, his lips descending on hers softly at first and then with the longing, the need, he felt for her. Finally breaking the kiss, he slipped his good arm around her shoulders and pulled her close.

"I think I'm going to have to talk to your father, then," Will said with a smile.

Katie wrapped her arm around his waist. "We'll go together."

Joshua James was waiting on the front porch when Katie and Will walked out of the bunk house together. The other men, seeing Katie enter, had vacated the place and come running to tell him that the two young people were there alone. He smiled watching them approach, Will leaning heavily on Katie as he hobbled along on his sore leg.

"Mr. James?" Will's voice was strong as he stepped up to the boss. "I've come to speak to you about asking your daughter to marry me." Will paused, waiting for any reaction, but when none came he carried on.

"I know I don't have much, but I promise to do my best to take care of her and provide for her. It might take a while, but eventually I'll have my own spread and …." His voice trailed off as the other man raised his hand to stop him, and a silence settled over the night.

"Son. Do you love her?" Joshua asked.

"Yes, sir," Will replied. Looking down into Katie's upturned face he said the words again. "I love her."

Katie's face was radiant in the soft light of a rising moon.

Joshua James stood to his full and impressive height, looking Will directly in the eye, and extended his hand.

"Welcome home," he said, shaking his soon to be son-in-law's hand.

Chapter 13

The last two weeks of August were a whirlwind of activity and excitement as preparations for a fall wedding were in full swing. Katie and Will were more than happy to just have a simple ceremony right away, but Nona was having none of that. She was beside herself with excitement and was determined to see everything done right for her Katie. She insisted on a 'real' wedding and nagged Joshua until he agreed to send one of the men to Casper for the preacher. She then threw herself into planning and preparation, even going so far as to send someone to Brion to invite him down for the festive event.

Katie and her sisters were put to work sewing a wedding dress, which Katie insisted that she didn't need, but secretly delighted in. Even Cathleen, who turned out to be a wizard with needle and thread, joined in, and in no time a beautiful gown of pale gold was complete. "Nona," Katie said one afternoon leaning over to kiss her grandmother's soft plump cheek. "You'd think you were the one getting married," Katie laughed. Nona's face lit up with delight.

"I love weddings," the matron said with a brilliant smile. "I always cry." Her eyes sparkled as she looked around the room at each of the girls. "Maybe this will be the first of many." Her smile was significant.

"Oh, Nona," Fiona said with a grimace. "How in the world are we to meet any young men all the way out here?"

130

The twins tittered. "Well, Katie did," Issy said with a gleam of delight in her eyes.

"I suppose we could talk Pa into shipping us all back East to find husbands," Lexi added mischievously, and winked at her twin.

"You are not going anywhere." Nona's voice was grim and at the horrified look on her face, the girls stopped there teasing and ran to her.

"We won't leave you, Nona," Fiona said from among the throng, wrapping an arm around her grandmother's shoulders. "I for one am perfectly content right here."

All the girls took their turns reassuring the woman who had loved and nurtured them all of their lives as if they were her own, managing to stem the tears that threatened to spill from her eyes. Nona patted each girl on the cheek and kissed them.

Now with a bright smile on her face, she rose from her chair and walked to where Katie's wedding dress lay draped across a chair, running her hand across it and admiring the work her granddaughters had done.

Will took full advantage of the time afforded him to court Katie properly. Each evening after supper he would collect Katie and together they would walk around the ranch talking quietly arm in arm, or sit on the porch swing and discuss ideas for their future.

Katie, like her father, was full of ideas about how the ranch should progress, and together they discussed how to diversify and move away from a total dependency on cows for their income. The ranch was already self-sufficient, but if they wanted it to be so down the road and for future generations decisions, would have to be made now.

Will reveled in her quick mind and how he could share his thoughts with her so easily. He also enjoyed stealing a kiss at every opportunity. When she wasn't busy working with Nona on wedding plans, Katie would occasionally ride out with Will, checking cattle or just looking at the ranch, but mostly just to be with him.

Will had taken to riding the ornery bay again and the horse had settled down fairly well under his steady hand. The weather was getting cooler now and in the high reaches of the mountains the peaks were dusted with snow.

It was only two days until the wedding and the soon-to-be weds were riding along the valley, keeping an eye out for any problems, when a few whiffs of dust across a gulley caught their eye. Laying heels to their mounts, they galloped toward the area to discover Katie's uncle and his family riding along. They had several animals with them, a few ewes and lambs and even a small string of ponies.

"Uncle Brion!" Katie called, excitedly waving as she drew up alongside her uncle and greeted her aunt and cousins.

Her petite aunt sat on a stout brown mare and looked at her knowingly, a smile playing across her dark features. Will smiled at the woman's expression, remembering the conversation from just a few weeks ago.

"I tell you," Wynonna Blakey said smugly.

Katie giggled, while Winny kicked her mare into a trot. The rotund animal stepped up its pace, revealing a spindly-legged blaze-faced foal that had been walking at her side. The creature was obviously only a few months old; its fuzzy coat was a deep liver brown with fluffy white mane and tail. The blaze that ran from just beneath the forelock to the end of his nose was wide, and he had one blue eye with a white rim. Will smiled at the little creature, noting the good legs and wide rump.

"You like him?" Brion's question caught him by surprise, and he turned toward the Irishman, a question in his eye.

"That colt? Do ya like him lad?" Brion asked, pointing toward the animal as it trotted along beside its mother once again.

"Yes, sir. That's a fine looking colt," Will replied with admiration in his voice.

"Good," Katie's uncle replied gruffly, "because he's a wedding present."

Will was so shocked he pulled his own mount up short, only to then kick the bay into a trot to catch up with Brion who continued laughing the whole time.

"His mother's the last of my blood stock I brought along here with me, and she's too old to stay up in those mountains, not to mention this colt came late. So Winny and I agreed we'd bring them down here where they'd both have a better chance of survival, and this youngster would be a fittin' present for ya."

Will's voice constricted in his throat and he couldn't speak. The little liver chestnut was probably the best stock Brion had, and he was giving him to Will.

Katie, seeing the emotion on his face, moved her palomino to his side and took his hand.

"It's what family does," she whispered softly, smiling up at him.

The wedding day broke clear and bright with a bustle of activity. Nona and Chen Lou laid out a breakfast fit for a king, then began chivying everyone on the ranch into various jobs in preparations for the ceremony.

Katie didn't have a moment to herself as all five of her sisters fussed about, helping her dress and do her hair. She wasn't even afforded any privacy in her bath. Meg was beside herself, spouting every kind of romantic nonsense she could think of, until all of the girls collapsed in peals of laughter.

Finally dressed and ready for the big moment, Katie stood and took a deep breath, her sisters all gathered around her. A soft knock on the door announced her father, and with a quick kiss from each, her sisters dashed from the room.

"You look like yer' ma," Joshua said, "absolutely beautiful." His smile was bright, but his eyes held subtle shadows; a father's memories of his little girl.

Katie ran into his arms.

"Oh, Pa! I'm so happy. I never dreamed it could ever happen, but here it is my wedding day."

With a chuckle he offered her his arm, and together they walked down the stairs, out onto the long back porch, and into the yard.

Will stood in his best suit of clothes under a large cotton wood tree. Isadore had built a small arbor which the girls had decorated with flowers and ribbons.

At the sound of the screen door opening, he looked up to see Katie descending from the porch on her father's arm. The sight of her took his breath away. She wore a gown of pale gold with soft white lace at her collar and cuffs. Her hair, the color of rose gold, shimmered in the late morning sun and her whole being seemed to glow. Their eyes met, and as he watched her walk toward him, all of the other people seemed to fade away like wraiths.

Moments later Joshua was laying Katie's hand in his. Will watched as the most beautiful woman on earth received a kiss on the cheek from her father, then turned toward the parson who had begun speaking. Will wasn't sure what the man said but somehow he was able to give the right responses, his heart thundering in his chest as Katie said the words to him. Katie's soft words faded as he gazed into her eyes, until finally the words he'd been waiting for came from the preacher.

"You may now kiss the bride," the wiry little man said, and Will reached for Katie, wrapping his arms tight around her slim waist and pulling her to him he lowered his head, pressing his lips to hers, willing his kiss to show her that she was his everything. She was his home.

Nona had outdone herself with the wedding supper. She'd had the men working for days to set up the arbor and tables. She, Billy, Chen Lou and the other girls had cooked and baked and sewed until everything was perfect.

A side of beef, roasted whole on a heavy spit over a banked fire, and dishes of all kinds covered the tables as everyone bowed their head for the grace. Joshua looked down the long table at each smiling face. He noted the sweet smiles of his daughters and the joy of every man of the Broken J. His eyes lingered on his oldest child as she sat next to her new husband and he smiled, then bowed his head.

"Dear Lord." His voice was soft but clear; reverent. "Thank you for this fine day and the many blessings you've given to each of us. Thank you for bringing these two young people together and for sharing your love with each of us here today. I ask your blessing on this union today and pray that you will grant them love, patience and understanding for the years ahead. Amen."

He lifted his eyes to the hushed table. Nona sniffed and everyone broke into laughter once more. At the end of the meal, Nona and Chen Lou brought out a beautiful cake and the men started tuning up their instruments. Soon the sound of laughter and music filled the whole space as the sun began to sink toward the horizon setting the sky ablaze in glorious reds, roses and gold.

Epilogue

Leaving the noise and laughter of the wedding supper behind him, Joshua James silently slipped away and glided under the heavy branches of the sprawling shelter of the old cottonwood tree. Removing his hat, he laid a dark hand on the pale gray head stone.

"I guess that's one down, darlin'," he said, a soft smile playing along his lips. "I'm afraid things didn't go exactly to plan, but in the end it all worked out. I've never seen Katie look more beautiful or happy. I reckon you knew what you were doing when you made me promise."

He smiled again and patted his breast pocket, causing it to crackle. "I guess it's time to get started again." Easing himself down into the deep green grass, he removed the letter that he'd been carrying with him since he'd left Casper, and ripped off the end. The crisp white velour page slid into his hand, and unfolding it, carefully he began to read.

Dear Joshua,
August 1, 1888

It has taken some time but I believe I've found exactly what you've been looking for here in Illinois. The item is used and is rather special though perhaps somewhat the worse for wear. It does not come as a single piece but with additional baggage. Still, it should fit well with the needs of the ranch. The packaging is perhaps a bit bulkier than you'd like but I'd place a high value on its worth. It should travel well and reach you sometime in October, if all goes to plan. I hope that it is received happily by everyone as it is sent to you with love.

Things are the same here in the city. I'm hoping with the elections coming up in November, perhaps we will finally find some relief from the trials and corruption of this once great place. Give my love to each of the girls and keep well.

Your loving brother,

Jonas

***

Bianca Leoné set the coffee pot back on the stove, placed a plate of molasses cookies on the table, and took her seat next to her husband, who turned up the lamp. It was late. Everyone else had turned in hours ago, Katie and Will having retired early to the bedroom they would now share.

Joshua James sat at the head of the kitchen table, a crisp white sheet of paper in his hand as he gazed around the group assembled there. The white of the paper and envelope seemed brighter in the deep darkness of the night.

"I received a letter from my brother, Jonas," Joshua said without preamble. "He's sending us a package." He paused, looking around the table significantly. "It should arrive sometime next month. He's a little cryptic when it comes to details. I know we agreed there would be no specifics, but that leaves something to be desired. Of course this last endeavor worked out for the best, so I guess we'll just have to have faith that the next one will go as well."

Billy's chuckle from the other side of the table made everyone look up. "I reckon' you can say it worked out alright but, ya' can't say it went off without a hitch." He chuckled again shaking his head. "Reckon, we'll just have to wait and see what happens next."

"I'll speak to the rest of the men before Cathleen and I leave for the cabin tomorrow," Benji said, reaching out and taking his wife's hand. "If you need anything more, we won't be far away."

Cathleen's soft eyes and bright smile twinkled as she suppressed a giggle. The whole clandestine meeting was almost more than her cheerful disposition could bear, but she understood the reasons that some secrets on the ranch were not shared equally.

"I'd say you all know what to do, but for now all we can do is wait and watch."

"And pray," Bianca added softly, before she stood and blew out the lamp.

For other books by this author check out the Author page at amazon.com/author/danni-roan

OR visit me at https://www.facebook.com/danniroan1/?ref=bookmarks

AND

If you enjoy Sweet Western Historical Romance take the time to look at https://www.facebook.com/groups/pioneerhearts/ a great place to find works in this genre.

For a sneak peek of the next book in The Cattleman's Daughters series go to the next page.

Made in the USA
Charleston, SC
15 June 2016